WAVE

WAVE

ERIC
WALTERS

**DOUBLEDAY
CANADA**

Doubleday Canada and colophon are registered trademarks.

Library and Archives Canada Cataloguing in Publication

Walters, Eric, 1957–
    Wave / Eric Walters.

ISBN 978-0-385-66443-1

    1. Indian Ocean Tsunami, 2004—Juvenile fiction.
I. Title

PS8595.A598W39 2009   jC813'.54   c2009-904025-5

Printed and bound in the USA

Published in Canada by Doubleday Canada,
a division of Random House of Canada Limited

Visit Random House of Canada Limited's website:
www.randomhouse.ca

10 9 8 7 6 5 4

For my editor, Amy Black, who not only believes in my books, but makes them better.

S
A
M

CHAPTER ONE

—

"I just can't believe that you're not coming with us," my mother said to my sister.

We were in the car on our way to the airport, but this time only three of the four of us were bringing luggage.

"I'll be with you in spirit," my sister answered.

"Spirit isn't the same thing, Beth. It's just going to—"

"Seem so strange," I said, cutting her off. If I'd let her finish, it would have made about the eleven *millionth* time she'd said that.

"Yes. It *will* be strange," my mother agreed. "Christmas without both of my kids with me will be . . . well, *worse* than strange. It'll be just . . . awful!"

"You're going to make her feel even more guilty than she already does, Ingrid," my father said. "Sooner or later this was going to happen. Children do grow up."

"Well, of course they do, but I wasn't expecting it to happen so soon." My mother's voice sounded teary.

"Beth, can you slow down a bit?" my father said.

"Not really, Dad. I mean, it's like you said, I am growing up, and—"

"I meant your driving," my father explained. "Can you slow down? The roads are a little slick." Beth was driving, and being in the passenger seat was not a comfortable place for my father.

"Yes, Father," my sister answered, in that formal tone she always used when she was sure he was wrong but she was prepared to humor him.

She slowed the car down. I was grateful. I knew she was a very responsible driver—a responsible *everything*—but I was never as easy going with her behind the wheel as when my father was driving. And the roads really were a bit icy—what else would you expect for December in New York?

"Besides," my mother said, "Beth's not the one who should be feeling guilty. *I'm* the one who's going to be lying in the sun and leaving my baby stuck up here in the snow and cold."

"I like the winter, Mom."

"But you *love* Phuket," my mother said. "You're always saying that Thailand is your favorite place in the world."

"Not anymore," I said.

They all looked at me quizzically—including my sister in the rearview mirror.

"Now her favorite is any place where her *Tadpole* is."

My father snorted a little and then choked back the laugh. "Tadpole" was the nickname I'd hung on Beth's boyfriend, Tad. She didn't like it, which of course made my father and me like it even more. They'd been together almost six months now, and it was beginning to look like a serious sort of thing.

"You all know that Tad has nothing to do with my decision to stay home. He's not even going to be around the whole the time."

"He's not?" my mother asked.

"No. His family is heading up to Vermont to ski. They go skiing every Christmas the same way we go to Thailand."

"I didn't know that," my mother moaned.

"I didn't tell you because I was sure, if you thought I was going to be alone for even a day, you'd want to cancel your trip and you'd end up ruining everybody's Christmas."

"So this way it's just *your* Christmas that's ruined?" my mother said.

"It won't be ruined," Beth said. "Tad's parents even invited me to come along with them."

"And you turned them down?" my father asked.

"I would have liked to go, but I couldn't."

"Why not?" my mother asked.

"For the same reason I can't go with you. They're not getting back until the twenty-eighth, and by then I have to be in Minnesota."

We all knew what that meant. Beth's swim team was heading out on the road for a swim meet on December 27.

My sister was in first-year university on a swimming scholarship.

"That is so stupid," I said to her. "Couldn't your coach find a swim meet in Alaska? How did he manage to find a meet in one of the few places in the entire United States that's even colder than New York?"

"I would have preferred Hawaii," she admitted. "Or Thailand."

"I just wish that my baby didn't—"

"I just wish that everybody would forget it!" Beth said, cutting her off sharply. "I'm not a baby, I'm a woman. I would rather have gone on vacation with my family, or even Tad's family, over Christmas, but it can't be. Tad's almost as bad as you—he offered to not go with his family so he could be here to babysit me. Honestly, everybody, I will be fine!"

We drove in silence for a while, the only sound the beating of the windshield wipers as they cleared away the snow.

Finally, Beth said, almost as an apology, "I really do wish I could go with you."

"It's the end of a family tradition," my mother said with a sigh.

Going to Thailand for Christmas was something my mother's family had been doing since long before Mom even met Dad. When Dad came along he joined in, and then when Beth and I were born we became part of the tradition too.

"It's just so sad," my mother said. "One after the other."

I knew what she was thinking about. I just hoped she wasn't going to cry. This was going to be the second Christmas since her mother died. Her father had passed on two years before that, so last Christmas had been the first with just the four of us . . . and this year there'd only be three.

"We'll call you," my mother said.

"If we can get a line," my father warned.

He was right to mention that. Phuket was beautiful—maybe the most beautiful place in the whole world—but the phone service could be a little sketchy. Especially at the small resort where we always stayed. It was on an island, a wonderful place, but there were no televisions or computers. They'd put phones in the little bungalows where we stayed only two years earlier. It was sort of like the Land That Time Forgot. My mother called it Paradise, and apparently Paradise came without broadband wireless, Internet, or reliable cellphone reception.

Usually my father liked that. It was his chance to get away from the world—more specifically, to get away from his law firm. Christmas in Thailand was the one time he could leave his BlackBerry behind and not have the office calling and pestering him about his clients. But being out of touch this year wasn't going to be such a bonus. It wouldn't have been nearly as hard on my parents to leave Beth behind if they could have been tethered by a telephone line. They were worried about her.

That almost made me laugh—like they really thought they had to worry about my sister. She was, without a doubt, the most responsible nineteen-year-old in the world. She didn't smoke or drink—not even a beer or a glass of wine. She was an honors student who had never skipped a class or failed a course—she'd never even had a grade below the high 80s. She was always where she was supposed to be, and on the rare occasions she couldn't be, she called. She helped around the house. She made meals and cleaned up without being asked. All of my parents' friends just *loved* her. She was on a full athletic scholarship, so even though my parents could easily have afforded to send her to school, she was there for free. Even her choice of boyfriend was perfect: Tad was in law school, he came from a good family, and he had a wonderful future in front of him. My sister was, in other words, probably the worst older sister a twelve-year-old guy could have.

I knew they tried not to compare the two of us, but it was just an inevitable, unspoken thing. I felt sort of like Supergirl's younger brother—no X-ray vision, couldn't fly, and was much slower than a speeding bullet. Not that I was a problem for my parents—I did well in school and sports and I had lots of friends—but I was no superhero fighting crime or evil super-villains, either.

Beth slowed the car down as we entered JFK International Airport. "Which terminal?"

"Three. Thai Airways," my father said. "Are you going to drop us off or come inside?"

"I'm going to park. I want to come inside and see you off—you know, wave goodbye."

My mother reached over from the back seat and gave Beth's shoulder a little squeeze.

"Just go to short-term parking," my father said. "I want you back on the road before the weather gets any worse."

"I'll be fine," Beth said.

"I know you'll be fine. Just indulge me on this, okay?"

My sister swung into a parking space. My father got out and fed the meter and I climbed out to start getting the luggage out of the trunk. It was cold and the wind was whipping the snow around. It probably wasn't falling as much as it was blowing. My father came around to help with the luggage while my sister offered my mother her arm and helped her toward the shelter of the terminal. I watched her move, slowly but steadily. I was looking for some telltale sign that it was starting to pass again, or that her symptoms were getting worse.

"She's going to be okay," my father said.

"I know. Beth can take care of herself."

"I meant your mother."

Why did it still surprise me that he could read my mind?

"She's already going into remission. I can tell," he said.

I wanted to believe him. I really did.

He pulled the last of the bags out of the trunk and we started to wheel them into the terminal. I tried to move quickly. It was cold and I wasn't dressed for it. None of us was, except Beth. We always left our winter coats and boots behind rather than take them with us on these trips. Better a mad dash in the cold than looking like a bunch of Eskimos lost in the tropics when we arrived.

My mother had navigated the slippery path without falling. She hadn't fallen in days. Maybe my father was right, but I just couldn't tell. Multiple Sclerosis was tricky like that. There were so many little symptoms—being tired, dropping things, losing your balance. Those things happened to everybody sometimes—no big deal—but in an MS sufferer they could mean the disease was getting worse. We'd learned that Multiple Sclerosis is an autoimmune disease that affects your body's whole central nervous system. My mother's type of MS was called "relapsing-remitting." She could have an episode and then, almost like magic, all the symptoms might fade away, and it would be like she didn't even have MS, or like she was cured. It could be that way for months. Once it had lasted almost two years. I'd even forgotten she had it that time.

My sister, though, never forgot. Even during the healthy times, the remissions, she was always there, watching, taking care of things, waiting for the relapse, when the symptoms would come back. Sometimes she seemed more like my mother's mother. Which of course meant that she was acting like *my* mother . . . or my grandmother . . . or whatever. Anyway, instead of acting like a big sister, which would have been bad enough, she was more like a third parent.

After passing through the sliding doors and into the terminal, I stomped my feet to shake the snow and slush off my sneakers. Wet feet for a twenty-five-hour plane trip was not an appealing thing.

"That is always the coldest two minutes of the winter," I said absently.

"Second coldest," Beth said. "Coming back to the car at the end of the trip is worse."

She had a point.

"Easy for you to say," I told her. She looked all warm and snuggly in her ski jacket and leather boots and gloves.

"That's the one and only tiny advantage of missing out on a tropical holiday with my family."

"Hey, it was your choice, so you're wasting your time if you think you can make me feel the *least* bit guilty." I started to walk away.

"Sorry. Wait," she said, and she grabbed me by the arm to slow me down. Mom and Dad were walking ahead. "Sam, I need you to help out Dad," she said.

"What does Dad need help with?"

"Watching Mom, of course!"

While she hadn't said, *Watching Mom, of course*, you idiot! that was clearly what she was actually saying.

"She's doing okay," I said. "She's in remission again."

"I don't know about that."

"Dad says—"

"Dad can never be trusted about that. He sees what he wants to see, and he only tells us what he thinks will make us feel better. Haven't you figured that out by now?"

"*I* think she's in remission, too."

"You're not much better than him."

"Thanks a lot." I paused. "So, you *don't* think she's in remission?"

"I don't know . . . maybe . . . yeah, I think probably."

"Then why are you giving me a hard time?" I demanded.

"I just want you to watch. And help. Make sure she doesn't have to carry anything heavy, or if you pour her a glass of water make sure it isn't too full. Offer a hand going down stairs—"

"I understand," I said. "I'll help where I can."

"Good. It's not fair to Dad if he has to do everything."

And maybe it wasn't fair to ask a twelve-year-old to take care of his mother. But, then again, what was fair about MS?

We swiftly caught up to Mom and Dad in the lineup at the ticket counter. We really didn't have to wait in line. My mother had a letter from her doctor explaining her condition, which would have allowed her—and her family, of course—to skip the lineup and pre-board the plane. But my mother wouldn't have any of that. She insisted on never taking advantage of her situation. She said if she were in a wheelchair it would be different. I hoped it would never be different. At least not for a long, long time. I knew where the MS road could lead—unable to walk, confined to a wheelchair, not able even to hold a glass, or dress herself. I just hoped it would be a slow trip with lots of stops along the way, and plenty of times when the whole train would turn around and head back toward total health.

We slowly shuffled forward, pushing and pulling our luggage along with us. The line was long but it was moving fairly quickly. We got to the front and a ticket agent waved us over.

"Welcome to Thai Airways. Four?" she asked.

"I wish," my mother said. "Just three." She placed our tickets and passports on the counter and the agent took them.

"How many bags?" the ticket agent asked.

"Three to check and three carry-on bags," my father said. He put the first two bags on the scale and I added the third.

"Did you pack the bags yourself, and have they been out of your care since you packed them?" she asked.

"We packed them, and they've been with us at all times," my father said.

The agent put tags on the three bags. She then handed back the tickets and passports. "Boarding is at nine-thirty so you should head through Security within the next fifteen minutes."

"Thanks," my mother said.

We walked along, my father leading, my mother with her arm around my sister's shoulders.

"One more thing," my father said. "I've left you a list of emergency contacts and my bank card . . . you know the PIN, right?"

"Of course, but I really don't need your bank card," she said.

"Just in case of an emergency. Suppose the car needed to be fixed, or there was some sort of problem at home like the furnace breaking. I'm sure nothing will go wrong, but just to be sure . . . okay?"

"Okay."

"I wish you were coming with us," Dad said, "but it's good to know that if anything goes wrong we can count on you to take care of it."

"You are so responsible," my mother added, giving my sister a little hug. "Now remember, we'll call you as soon as we get there."

"Best to call me on my cellphone. I'm not planning on spending much time in my room."

"Your room?"

"At the dorm. I'm going to go back to school tomorrow."

"But you don't have to be back at school until the twenty-seventh, do you?" my mother asked.

"No, but I just can't see staying at home all that time by myself. At least at school there are a few people still around. Some kids live too far away to go home for the holidays. And of course there are the international students, too. There are even a couple of members of the swim team who are sticking around over the holidays. At least I won't be completely alone."

My mother made a little gasping sound. God, she *had* almost made me feel bad.

"Honest, Mom, it's okay. We're going to have our own little Christmas gathering and everything. It'll be fine."

We stopped in front of the security gates.

"I think this is it," my father said.

My mother and then my father gave my sister a hug goodbye. I could tell that my mother was working hard at not crying. She wasn't doing that good a job.

"Aren't you going to give your sister a hug?" my father asked.

"If I have to," I protested. I wrapped my arms around her.

"Wow, when did you get so big?" she asked.

"It's not that I'm getting bigger—I think you're shrinking. Maybe it's all that time in the pool."

"I don't think so." She gave me another hug. "Help Dad, don't forget," she whispered in my ear.

"I will," I whispered back. "Don't worry."

"We have to get going," my father said.

My mother gave Beth another quick squeeze and then we started for the security gates.

We stopped just before we entered and I looked back. My sister gave a little wave. I waved back. And then she turned and walked away.

CHAPTER TWO

—

Our taxi slowed down and came to a stop in front of the resort.

"It feels like coming home," my mother said.

"Home for the holidays," my father agreed.

We climbed out of the car and the driver got out and took the bags from the trunk. Instantly there were three bellhops who grabbed them.

"I love the smell of the air here," my mother said.

"I just like the fact that the air is warm." I rolled up the sleeves on my shirt. The faster I could get into a T-shirt and shorts the better. Actually, a bathing suit would be even better.

"Hello, Mr. and Mrs. Brooks!"

It was Philippe. He'd worked at the resort for as long as I could remember.

"It's so good to see all of you . . . but it isn't all of you. Where is Miss Brooks?" he asked.

"Miss Brooks couldn't come this year," my mother said.

"That is awful!" Philippe exclaimed. "The staff will be so disappointed."

I knew he was, in a way, just being polite. The Thai people had to be the most polite in the entire world. But he also really meant it. Over the years we'd gotten to know the staff, and they'd gotten to know us. They really worked to make our stay as enjoyable as possible. They didn't have to work at being friendly, though, because that part just came naturally.

My father started to pick up one of our suitcases and Philippe practically grabbed it out of his hand. He barked out some orders in Thai and three other staff came running. Philippe handed one of them my father's bag and the other two grabbed the rest.

"You are, of course, in the best location at the resort, bungalow number six," Philippe said.

We'd been in bungalow six for the past five years. For four years before that we'd had bungalow two, but six was better because it was at the end of the beach, farthest away from the main resort building. It felt like our own little cottage. When it had first become available my father had grabbed it up, and now we had a standing reservation for every Christmas.

"You all must be hungry," Philippe said. "I had a meal prepared for you and it is waiting on the patio."

My mother gave Philippe a hug. "You always take such good care of us. You make us feel like family."

"Some people who come are only guests. Others *are* family. Come."

Philippe led the way. That wasn't really necessary. I knew this resort halfway around the world better than almost anywhere else on earth.

We trailed behind him and into the hotel's main lobby. As we passed the desk, the two clerks there waved and called out greetings. My father went over and shook hands with both of the men. I did the same. They, too, were disappointed that my sister wasn't with us. It kind of made me feel worse about it.

"Come, your meal is waiting," Philippe said.

We continued through the lobby, past the little waterfall, past the dining room, and out onto the patio, which overlooked the pool and then the beach. The shimmering sand was almost white. Beyond that was the ocean. It was so spectacular it always took my breath away. There were a few sailboats out, their brilliant colors contrasting with the deep blue of the water, and beyond that were the village fishing boats coming in with their morning catch. There wasn't even a cloud to stain the rich blue sky. It all looked like a postcard.

There were a few hotel guests in the pool, and a few more were lying around in lounge chairs. Beyond that, the beach looked nearly empty. I figured there were people out there, but they were hiding in their cabanas, resting or reading or sleeping. That was my plan—to go out there and have a midday nap.

To the far left, directly on the beach, were the hotel bungalows. Lots of people liked to stay in the hotel itself but we always stayed in the bungalows. For one thing, you were right there on the ocean, not separated from it by a set of stairs or a lobby or even much sand. You could just run right out and jump into the water. And best yet, because our bungalow was the farthest away from the hotel, we had the most privacy of anyone. It almost felt like we were in our own little world when we were down there.

On the patio, Philippe stopped at a table and pulled out a chair for my mother while Dad and I sat down. Without even being called, two waiters magically appeared carrying trays. They set two big bowls of fresh fruit in front of my parents, and in front of me one of them placed an enormous stack of pineapple pancakes! The table was set for four, and they were ready to set down pancakes at Beth's place, but Philippe waved them away. Quickly, wordlessly, he gathered up her place setting.

"I hope they're still your favorite," Philippe said.

"They are! All I need is some syrup."

Almost before I could get the words out, one of the waiters set down a pitcher of golden syrup in front of me.

"Please, enjoy your meal," Philippe said.

"This all looks so wonderful!" My mother beamed. "Right after we eat, we can go for a walk along the beach or—"

"Or lie down and rest for a while," my father said.

"I feel fine."

"Maybe *I* need to rest," my father responded. "How about you, Sam?"

"I slept on the plane so I'm feeling pretty—" Then I clued in that that wasn't the answer he wanted. "Yeah, actually, a nap would be good . . . although I was hoping to take a nap on the beach, in one of the cabanas."

"A cabana was reserved specifically for you to do that," Philippe said. "And I will arrange for your beds to be turned down in the bungalow."

"Philippe, you are amazing," my father said.

Philippe smiled. "If there is anything you need, you simply must ask." He bowed from the waist and then left.

"Can you smell the air?" my mother asked. "It's so, so . . . fresh!"

"It does smell lovely," my father agreed.

It was nice—especially when combined with the smell of pineapple pancakes and syrup—but it was nothing special. My mother's reaction had more to do with the fact that she hated the way New York smelled. It didn't bother me. The only time I really noticed was in the middle of the summer. Then it did kind of stink. It sort of reminded me of somebody's gym bag.

As we ate, I glanced up at my mother. She wasn't the best sleeper even at home, and she didn't seem to be able to sleep at all on planes. That made the trip down here that much harder for her. She looked tired, and I could see a slight tremor in her hand as she used her fork.

"I can't wait to get out for a quick dip," I said.

"But you will wait until I'm there, right?" my father said.

If he was going to nap, that might be hours. I didn't want to wait that long.

"How about if I just wade out a little?" I asked.

"How about if you wait?"

"Come on, Dad, it's not like I'm going to drown in two feet of water."

"I've heard of people drowning in their bathtubs," he countered.

"Okay, I'll make you a deal. I won't take any baths for the whole trip."

He laughed. Good sign.

"I won't go out far. You know how gentle the slope is here." The water wouldn't be over my head until I was at least twenty-five yards out from shore. "Besides, it's not like I can't swim."

"Even good swimmers should have a buddy," he said.

"Look who's talking!" I exclaimed.

My father smiled sheepishly. We all loved the water, but my father was the person who Beth got her swimming genes from. He could swim for hours. Every summer we took a cottage on Cape Cod. My father would just swim, paralleling the beach fifty yards out, for miles and miles on end.

"I've got an idea," my mother said. "Since I'm the only one who really needs to take a nap, how about you two go out and swim while I lie down?"

My father gave her a concerned look. "Are you sure?"

"I think I'll be okay taking a nap by myself. My two boys should just enjoy themselves. Come and wake me up when it's time to go for dinner."

I stretched out on the lounge chair. My father was asleep in the chair beside me. Apparently my mother wasn't the only one who needed a nap. The canvas of the cabana gave us protection from the sun, but there was no wind, and the heat was building. It had to be over ninety degrees. The only relief would be another dip in the ocean.

I got up and made a quick run across the open beach, the sand burning the bottoms of my feet until I reached the water. It was cooler than the sand, but still pretty warm. It felt more like taking a bath than swimming in an ocean. I waded out a dozen feet, the water just above my knees, and then slumped down so my whole body was under the water as I sat on the bottom, the waves bobbing me up and down. It was important not to be directly exposed to the sun in the first few days. My sister had done that once and paid the price—a bad burn that almost ruined the rest of her trip.

I sat there looking out at the ocean. It was a brilliant bluish-green color, so beautiful that it almost didn't seem real. I wasn't much for looking at scenery, but that ocean view was really something.

As far as I could see in either direction there were only a few other people in the water and a few more on the beach. That wasn't unusual. The heat and sun in the middle of the day drove people off the beach and into the shade. People who wanted to be in the water would often sit in the pool instead, shaded by umbrellas, and order drinks or snacks from the bar. I had nothing against a cold drink—actually, I could have gone for a Coke right about then—but there was something pretty amazing about being in the ocean. There was something pretty amazing about just being here.

In one short day we'd come halfway around the world. We'd left behind the cold and snow and crowds and concrete of New York City and landed on a sunny, hot beach at a tropical island resort. It was like another world.

I got up and ran across the blazing-hot sand to the cabana, where I plopped back down in the lounge chair. My father let out a big yawn and stretched and then opened his eyes.

"What time is it?" he asked.

"I don't know. I left my watch behind at home with my ski jacket. I think it's about five."

"Five? That would mean I was sleeping for almost four hours."

"Not just sleeping. You were *snoring* for four hours. I don't know how Mom puts up with you."

"I've wondered the same thing myself. By the way, I'm thinking that she and I are going to have a pretty low-key day tomorrow . . . hang around, eat, maybe have a massage and do a little shopping."

"Sounds incredibly exciting," I said sarcastically.

"A little peace and quiet suits me fine," he said, stretching his arms over his head.

"So what am *I* supposed to do?" I asked. "The only thing in the world that I'd like to do less than shop is have a massage."

"I understand. What would you like to do tomorrow instead?"

"I haven't really thought about it. I guess I could just hang around too."

"You could, but you don't have to." He paused. "There's no need for both of us to watch your mother."

"But there is a need for you to, right?"

"The trip is long and hard on her. She just needs a slow day to regain her strength and she'll be fine. She always rebounds, you know that."

I knew it. And as long as each relapse was followed by a remission, it didn't matter. But that didn't stop me from worrying every time there was a relapse.

"So, tell me, instead of hanging around, what *would* you like to do?" he asked again.

"I don't know . . . I guess I was hoping to do something with you and Mom. Isn't there something we could do together that wouldn't be too tiring? Maybe we could go for a boat ride, or . . . ." Then it came to me. "What about if we went on an elephant ride? We've never done that before."

"You've ridden an elephant before."

"I don't mean a little ride on the beach. I mean a full tour up into the hills."

"That sounds like a good idea. We take it easy in the morning and we go on a tour in the afternoon?"

"Works for me!"

He reached over and we shook hands. "Deal."

CHAPTER THREE

—

I looked at my wrist where my watch was supposed to be. There was nothing but a couple of freckles and the remnants of my summer tan line showing the spot it usually occupied. Even the tan line would be gone after a few days in the sun. No one in our family ever wore a watch while we were in Thailand. We were officially on "Thai Time." It was tradition, and it certainly was symbolic, but it could be a pain. Sometimes you just had to know the real time. Like, for example, when you were supposed to be meeting your family for an elephant ride.

I looked around at the other tourists lounging around the pool. There were a lot of them, but nobody seemed to be wearing a watch. Nobody was wearing anything more than a bathing suit. Actually, I would have been happier if some of them had been wearing towels.

Why was it that all European men thought they should wear a little skimpy Speedo? No matter how fat they were, they paraded around in nothing but tiny bathing suits and flip-flops. Some of the men had bellies that were so big and hung down so low you couldn't even see the thin scrap of fabric, which made them look like they were naked. I shuddered at the thought.

There *was* a nude beach just down the way, a stretch of sand about half a mile from the resort, tucked into a little cove. When I'd first heard about it I'd suddenly understood why my parents were always so insistent on taking us on walks in the *other* direction. That made me even more curious, of course. I really, really had to go and look, so finally, I snuck off and had a peek. What a letdown! Clearly, there was some sort of mathematical equation at work. The less attractive somebody was, or the more overweight they were, the more likely they were to be there, walking around naked or playing volleyball on the beach. The few woman who were worth looking at were always lying face down, discreetly, on a towel.

I decided it was far better to spend some time getting to know the good-looking girls in cute bikinis around the hotel pool. Not that there were that many girls around the resort that I could imagine as girl-friends. It was more of a family and retired folks sort of resort. There were a few little kids, a lot younger than me, and a lot of people the age of my parents and up, plenty of them senior citizens, but I was virtually the only guy my age at the whole resort. It made me wish even more that my sister had been able to come. Even though she sometimes acted like a fussy old woman, she would at least have been somebody close to my age to hang around with.

None of this answered my question about time. I knew there was a clock behind the desk in the lobby, so I got up and strolled around the pool. People nodded or said hello as I passed. I didn't know any of them, but people who came here seemed to get infected by the Thai friendliness. In New York they would have just rushed by. Here, people seemed to have time to talk. There probably would have been even more conversation if more of them had spoken English.

I knew from the little snippets of conversation that I heard, and from past visits, that there were people here from dozens and dozens of countries. Not just from the United States and Canada, or England and Australia— places where they *sort* of spoke English—but from all over Europe. My mother's family was originally from Sweden—she even spoke a little Swedish—and there were lots and lots of people from Sweden here.

You could tell who the Swedes were without even asking. They were usually the ones playing volleyball or running on the beach. They looked athletic and were tall and often had whitish-blond hair. My mother and I both had hair like that. My father always joked that he could see himself in his dark-haired daughter, but nothing of himself in me. In fact, my mother and I looked so Swedish that sometimes a tourist would just walk up to one of us and start speaking Swedish. Mom knew enough that she could sort of communicate. I only knew a couple of words, including how to say "Hello" and "How are you?"—"*Halla dar*! *Vem ar ni*?"—and "Goodbye"—"*Adjo.*" That was about it. Luckily, it seemed like everybody in Sweden spoke at least some English. Actually, all the Europeans at the resort seemed to speak at least a little English as well.

I saw Philippe. He waved at me and came rushing over.

"I was just looking for you," he said. "Your elephant is waiting."

I laughed. That wasn't something I heard very often.

"I just have to find my parents."

"That is easy. They are already sitting on top of your elephant! Come!"

I ran after Philippe. He was tiny—I towered over him—but he moved very quickly. We cut through the lobby and out the front door. There, right by the entrance, standing among the waiting taxis, was the elephant. My parents were already sitting in the big wicker basket—the howdah—on its back.

"We thought you were going to miss it!" my father yelled out.

I ran up to the elephant. It had gleaming white tusks, and it was enormous—a lot bigger than the one down at the beach that was used for little two-minute rides for kids. A set of stairs was there to help me, and I climbed up. The driver—he was called a mahout—reached out and offered me a hand to help me over the gap, onto the elephant and then into the basket. I settled in right beside my mother.

"All right?" the mahout asked.

"Let's go," my father replied.

The mahout sat down in front of the basket so he was more on the head of the animal than the back. He said something to the elephant and it started to move, and we were all rocked forward.

"My name is Nija, I am the mahout, and my elephant is Ning."

"Good to meet you. We are Sam and James and Ingrid, the Brooks family," my father answered.

The elephant moved between one of the waiting taxis and a souvenir stall on the sidewalk. It was a tight squeeze but he didn't even nudge either of them.

"You have a beautiful elephant," my mother said.

"He is a fine elephant. Very smart. Very big. We have been together for many years."

"So you've been giving tours for a long time," my father said.

"Not long. Before, we worked in the forest. Ning is very strong, also."

"But you decided you wanted to do this instead?" my mother suggested.

"Government decided. No more cutting trees. Now give tours."

We moved along the side of the road. On one side there was a fairly constant parade of vehicles—some small cars, an occasional bus or a truck, and lots and lots of bicycles. On the other side was the sidewalk, and it was packed with people and stands selling everything from fresh fruit to fake fashions and Rolex rip-offs.

Some of the tourists on the sidewalk took pictures as we passed, but for the most part we were pretty much ignored. An elephant walking down the street almost anywhere else in the world—even in New York, where people pretended that nothing fazed them—would have drawn a little more attention. Here, it didn't mean much. There were lots of elephants. Some were just for the tourists, but others were used to haul things, pull wagons delivering merchandise to stores, or for roadside construction.

Nija yelled out something and the elephant cut across the road, weaving through cars and bicycles, which had to dodge out of his way. He then walked through a wooded area. I didn't even see a path, but the elephant threaded his way around the trees and bamboo thickets and started up a hill. We tilted backwards as the slope rose. I felt a little uneasy. The elephant seemed to be gaining speed, even though we were on a steeper angle. I risked a glance over the side. The ground below was littered with rocks and tree stumps. What if he fell or tripped? It wasn't as if we had seat belts or a roll bar or air bags or anything. We had only a little bamboo-and-wicker basket holding us in place. I was beginning to wish I'd asked for a little kiddie ride on the beach. Maybe, I thought, I could ask him to slow down a bit.

"This is fun!" my mother exclaimed.

Now there was no way I could say anything or I'd look like a complete wimp. Luckily for my stomach, the ground suddenly leveled off and we were in a big flat field. There were lots of trees—banana trees—and we were walking between the rows.

"Where exactly are we going?" I asked my father.

He shrugged. "Nija, where are we heading to?"

"Up through the rubber plantation and to the temple at the top of the hill."

"Sounds good," my father said.

"The temple is wonderful," my mother said. "Sam, do you have any sunscreen on?"

"Yeah, I put some on."

"Your nose looks red. Here, let me put on some more."

She reached into her bag and pulled out a tube. I had put some on earlier in the day, but not since I had been swimming. It couldn't hurt. She squirted a big blob into my hands and I rubbed it all around my face and neck. She did the same for my father and then herself. It wasn't as necessary for Dad. His dark hair and darker skin provided some relief. But for us two fair-skinned "Swedes" it was crucial.

The elephant settled into a slow, steady pace and we rocked gently on his back. It was interesting to see the banana trees from this angle, looking down. We were so close that I figured I could reach out and grab a banana. If my parents hadn't been right beside me I would have tried.

I couldn't help thinking about my sister. Here we were on the back of an elephant moving through a tropical forest, and she was stuck in the cold and snow. Then again, it was almost two in the afternoon here, so that meant it was one in the morning in New York. She was probably sleeping, or at least getting ready for bed. It wasn't so bad to be tucked away in a warm bed on a cold winter's night.

Nija called out to some people on a donkey cart coming toward us. They smiled and waved and yelled friendly greetings. As they passed, I realized that up here in the hills, only a short distance from the crowded beaches and resorts, we were almost completely alone. Those were the first people we'd met. This was a slice of Thailand that we didn't see too often. Down below, we were all cocooned in our little resorts, and most of the people were other tourists. The only Thais we'd see were the people working at the resort or selling us stuff from the roadside stands. I wondered what it would be like to take a holiday up here. How did somebody like Philippe live when he wasn't catering to us and the other tourists?

We'd left the banana trees behind and were now moving among tall, thin trees that were haphazardly planted. The spaces between the trees were overrun with weeds, and the whole area looked untended.

"This is the rubber plantation," Nija said.

"It looks deserted," my father commented.

"It is."

"But isn't rubber valuable . . . shouldn't the planta-tion still be worked?"

"These trees are too old. They don't produce enough gum," Nija told him.

My father turned to me and explained, "They tap the trees for gum to make rubber, the same way you get sap to make maple syrup in Vermont." He asked Nija, "Is rubber still one of the biggest industries in Thailand?"

"Yes, still important," Nija said. "But now most important are tourists."

I guessed that made sense. Here we were on top of an elephant that used to be used for industry. Now it was carting us around for our tourist money.

"How old is your elephant?" my mother asked Nija.

"Twenty-five."

That sounded pretty old. "How long do elephants live?" I asked.

"Fifty or sixty years."

"I didn't know that," my father said.

"Sometimes longer," Nija said. "A lot depends on how they are treated." He reached down and gave his elephant a pat on the head and wrapped his arms around him. "This elephant is going to live to be a hundred years old!"

I was really enjoying the ride now. There was a certain rhythm to the elephant's walk. It certainly was far from smooth, but it was steady and constant. We were rocked back and forth in a comforting way. It was kind of reassuring, lulling. I could almost imagine falling asleep.

Up ahead I could see that the trees ended at an open field, and beyond that was a large building with a peaked roof.

"Is that the temple?" I asked.

"That's it," my mother answered.

The closer we got, the bigger and more elaborate the building looked. There was a long path leading up to it through a manicured lawn, and statues—lots of statues.

"What's that smell?" I asked. It was like flowers or fruit, strong but nice.

"Incense. The monks are burning incense. I love that smell," my mother answered.

Nija brought the elephant to a stop before we reached the temple grounds. He called out to Ning, the elephant, who brought his trunk up, wrapped it around the mahout, and lowered him to the ground. For a split second I had a terrible fear that that was how we were all going to get down. Instead, Ning kneeled down. I was just about to climb down when I realized that what might be easy for me and my father might be nearly impossible for my mother.

"Is there another way down?" my father asked. Obviously he was thinking the same thing.

"I'll be fine," my mother answered. Apparently, we'd all had the same thought. "I'll be careful, and you two can help."

"I'll go first," my father offered.

He climbed past me and used the elephant's head and trunk like stairs, lowering himself to the ground. Next I helped my mother climb out of the basket and onto Ning's head. She seemed to be moving pretty steadily, but I held her arm tightly just to make sure. She sat down on Ning's head and I let go. Slowly she slid down the side of the elephant's head and into the waiting arms of my father.

"That was fun!" she exclaimed.

I followed after, and once we were all safe on solid ground we made our way toward the temple.

"This is pretty fancy," I said.

"This one is nowhere near as opulent as the Grand Palace," my mother said, "but still, it's my favorite."

"You've been here before?"

"I come up here every year."

"How come I didn't know about it?" I asked.

"You and your father would be out snorkeling or sailing and I'd come up here for a little quiet time. It's the best place in the world for thoughtful contemplation."

I wasn't exactly sure what that meant.

"Come. I'll show you around."

There was a long staircase leading up to a large front door—more like a gate than a door, really. As we started up the steps, the smell of the incense became stronger. It wasn't just that you could smell it, you could almost taste it. It made me feel hungry. The smell seemed to be dripping down the stairs to where we sat.

"Take off your shoes," my mother said quietly.

Just outside the door were a dozen or more pairs of well-worn sandals. We left our flip-flops there, and my mother led us into the temple.

It was a large, open space with a soaring ceiling. At the front was a big wooden altar, where the sticks of incense were burning. Behind that were five huge statues of Buddha. Then, in front of the statues, I saw a half dozen people, all on their knees on little straw mats. They were bowing, touching their heads to the ground.

"Should we be here?" I whispered.

My mother nodded her head. "The monks like to have visitors."

"Those people at the front . . . are they praying?"

"Possibly praying, probably meditating."

"Meditating?"

"Contemplating life, trying to find peace and inner harmony," she explained. "This is a place for quiet thought."

It was quiet. Very quiet. Eerily quiet. It was as if even the whispered sounds of our voices were absorbed by the walls, which were lined with hundreds and hundreds of smaller statues.

As we talked, the people at the front repeatedly bowed low, touching their foreheads to the ground. Occasionally they would rise, bow, and return to their knees again. Two Buddhist monks, dressed in brilliant orange, glided across the room. I was used to seeing them along the streets. They always looked contented, happy— sort of Buddha-like. They, too, bowed to the statue, and then they proceeded to light more incense sticks.

I looked up at the biggest Buddha statue, the one above and behind the center of the altar. His hands were together in his lap, his eyes closed. On his face was the same expression that was on every statue of Buddha I'd ever seen—that smile. It reminded me of the smile on the face of the Mona Lisa. It was as if the Buddha had just made a wonderful discovery, learned something very satisfying, something that answered a long-held question.

But with the Mona Lisa I always thought she was keeping the secret to herself. With the Buddha, it was like, if you politely asked and listened ever so intently, he'd share that wisdom with you. The only question was, what question should I ask?

CHAPTER FOUR

—

There was sweat dripping from Philippe's nose . . . or should I say *Santa Claus's* nose. Philippe was dressed in a heavy red Santa suit, complete with hat, black boots, and long white beard. Three of the other staff members were dressed as elves. Overnight, the palm trees had been festooned with Christmas lights and ornaments, and there was a blow-up scene of Santa and his reindeer on the roof of the pool cabana. They'd even set up a life-sized nativity scene by the poolside bar. It looked as though the three wise men were waiting for a cool drink—presumably nothing alcoholic.

The waiters were moving through the crowd with hot rum drinks for the adults and hot chocolate for the kids and wishing everybody a "merry Christmas." It was Christmas Day in Thailand. If the white sand had been white snow, the palm trees had been evergreens, and the temperature hadn't been hovering in the high nineties, it could have been Christmas morning back in New York City.

In some ways, I thought, the weather here was probably close to what it would have been like at the original Christmas in Bethlehem. At least, it was a lot more like it than some Hallmark-card moment with snow and a blazing fire. On the other hand, I knew that most of the people in Thailand were Buddhists and this probably didn't mean much to them, except as something else to please the tourists.

To most people back home this scene would have seemed surreal—a brilliant blue ocean in the background under a near-perfect sky framing a bright sun. But for me, this *was* Christmas. No cold or snow, skiing or skating, no chestnuts roasting on any fire helping to warm the winter weather. This was *our* Christmas, Christmas in Thailand. Okay, maybe just once it would have been nice to stay home, feel the cold, and play in the snow. That was the Christmas Beth was having this year. Her first Christmas at home.

Santa was in the process of calling up each guest and giving him or her a small present from his bag. Mine was a little key chain with a flashlight and a laser pointer, my father got a pen-and-pencil set, and my mother's gift was a silk scarf—all compliments of Santa . . . otherwise known as the hotel.

First thing that morning we'd also opened one present from each other. My father gave my mother a nice gold necklace, she gave him a digital camera, and my present was an iPod. The family rule was one present each, and it had to be something small enough to pack. The rest of the presents were at home in the living room under an artificial Christmas tree, waiting for our return.

"When should we try to call Beth?" I asked.

"Later today. Right now it's not even Christmas for her. It's still Christmas Eve," my father said.

"Maybe we should start to try now," my mother said. "Given the trouble with the phones, it might even be worthwhile to try to call her twice, once now and once when Christmas has arrived for her."

"That sounds like a plan," my father said. "I'll go and talk to the front desk and see if they can put a call through."

"I'll do it," I said as I quickly got to my feet.

"Don't you want to stay for the Christmas carols?" my mother asked. "They're just getting ready to start singing."

Yet another reason to leave. "I think I'll pass on that."

"You might ask them to try her cell number," my father said. "It's about ten in the evening so I'm sure she's out."

"Makes sense."

As I started away, Santa and the elves began to sing "Jingle Bells." The words were right but the rhythm was really off. Everybody sitting around the pool joined in and the rhythm seemed to correct itself.

"Merry Christmas!" the desk clerk sang out as I stopped at the counter.

"Merry Christmas."

Behind him was a life-size Santa Claus cutout. Santa looked very happy. Actually, take away the beard and he had an almost Buddha-like expression. Santa as Buddha . . . an interesting thought. One I wasn't going to be sharing with any Buddhists.

"I was hoping you could try to put through a telephone call."

"I can certainly try. But I have to apologize, I am not having much success today. Please, what is the number?"

I wrote down Beth's cellphone number and handed it to him.

"How long do you think it might take?" I asked.

"It could be a long time. I am still trying to connect a call to Chicago. It's been three hours."

"We'll be down by the pool if you get through."

"Thanks . . . and merry Christmas!"

"Yeah, merry Christmas."

I rolled over, awoken by the loud, sharp sound of a ringing telephone. I looked at the digital clock on the table. It was four in the morning. Who would be calling us now? I grabbed the receiver.

"Hello," I mumbled.

"We have a call for you from New York," the desk clerk said.

"A call . . . New York . . ." It had to be Beth, but why was she calling in the middle of the night? She had to know the time . . . something had to be wrong.

"Put it through."

The line buzzed and then clicked.

"Hello, Beth?"

"Sam, what's wrong?" Beth asked. "Has something happened to Mom?"

"Mom? She's sleeping . . . she's in bed. What's wrong in New York? Are you okay?"

"Of course I'm okay. Everything is fine here."

Then why had she called? Maybe she did have the time change confused and didn't realize how late it was . . . or early. "Beth, it's four in the morning here."

"I know the time. That's why I was so worried when I got the call."

"Got the call?" Then I realized what had happened. "Beth, we asked the hotel staff to try to place a call to you this afternoon, and they must have kept trying until they finally got you."

"They got me, all right. They scared me half to death."

"Everything is okay. Mom and Dad are sleeping."

She let out a big sigh. I knew Beth well enough to know how worried she would have been, but it wasn't like it was anybody's fault.

"We were just calling to wish you a merry Christmas," I said.

"It's not too late," she replied. "It's still Christmas here."

"What time is it?"

"Five. I'm just getting ready to go and have Christmas dinner."

I felt a rush of sadness. I could picture her sitting all by herself and—

"Tad drove down from Vermont to spend the afternoon with me," she said. "He's going back in a few hours, but we'll have dinner together!"

That was better!

"Hold on and I'll wake up Mom and Dad," I said.

"No! Mom shouldn't be disturbed. She needs her rest."

"Not as much as she needs to talk to you."

"You could just call back later," Beth suggested.

"It took sixteen hours to get this call through."

"I guess you're right."

"Besides, Mom would shoot me if I didn't wake her up. You know that. Hold on."

I put the phone down, flicked on a light, and ran to my parents' room. I knocked on the door and pushed it open.

"Mom . . . Dad . . ."

"Sam, are you okay?" my father asked.

"I'm fine. It's the phone. Beth is on the phone."

"Beth? It's the middle of the night . . . is something—?"

"Nothing's wrong," I said. "They just put through our call from this afternoon. Pick up the phone."

I ran back to my room. Behind me I saw the light from their bedside lamp. I grabbed the phone in time to hear them say hello and exchange Christmas greetings. Beth explained about Tad being with her and he chimed in a "Merry Christmas!" in the background. Tad had just come up a few notches in my books, and I figured he'd also won brownie points with my parents, as well.

"What's the weather like?" my father asked.

"It was a sunny day, but pretty cold," Beth said. "Apparently it snows at Christmas. Who knew?" she joked.

"Not anybody here," my father replied. "We had blue skies and temperatures in the mid-eighties. Christmas in Paradise."

"All right, that's enough, you don't have to rub it in!"

"So you and Tad are going out for dinner?" my mother asked.

"Not really out," Beth said. "All the restaurants are closed."

"You're not going to order in pizza, are you?" my mother asked.

"No, we're staying right here at the university."

"Cafeteria food? How awful."

"No, it's going to be a really nice meal," Beth said. "Most of the university is closed down for the holidays but they leave one cafeteria open, and they're serving a full turkey meal with cranberry sauce and the works."

"That sounds more like Christmas than anything we ever have here," I said. Our Christmas meal had been sweet-and-sour pork, rice, and curried goat.

"And then Tad has to get back up to his family," Beth said.

I could almost hear my mother's reaction. I could picture her pained expression, thinking that her little girl wasn't with her own family.

"So you'll be alone after that?" my mother asked.

W
A
V
E

"No, there are a lot of us around," Beth said. "Suzie and Meagan from the swim team are here, and there are a lot of other orphans around campus."

"You're not an *orphan*," my mother said. I couldn't tell if she sounded hurt, guilty, or offended.

"That's just what we're calling each other. It's a pretty big gang."

"So you're orphans, but the orphanage is full," my father joked.

"Pretty full."

"Did you open your present?" my father asked.

"It's beautiful! Thank you both so much!"

I had no idea what they'd given her.

"I picked it out myself," my father said.

That could have meant a new set of golf clubs, power tools, or a gift certificate from Macy's.

"I'm wearing them right now," Beth said.

That pretty well eliminated power tools and golf clubs, unless she had the golf bag over her shoulder.

"Your mother has the matching necklace," my father said.

"And it's beautiful too," she said. "He didn't even tell me that he got you the earrings until I opened my present."

"I couldn't tell either of you what I got the other without ruining the surprise," he said.

"So, Dad, nobody helped you pick these out?"

"I don't know why you should sound so surprised. It's not like I don't have taste."

I snorted.

"No comments from the peanut gallery," he said, laughing.

"I'm so impressed that you did it all by yourself," my mother said.

"Well . . ." Dad said, "not exactly all by myself."

"He didn't come looking to me for my fashion sense," I said.

"You don't *have* a fashion sense," Beth said.

"I did have some help from the salesgirl in Tiffany's," Dad admitted.

"Help?" Beth asked.

"I went in and told her I was buying Christmas presents for the two most wonderful and beautiful women in the world, and she took it from there."

"It's nice to know that at four in the morning you can still talk like a lawyer," my sister said.

"Not like a lawyer," he said. "Like a husband and father who knows how blessed he is."

"I think I'm going to be sick," I muttered on the extension.

"Blessed with the most wonderful son, as well," he added.

"Keep that in mind the next time I do something wrong."

There was some noise in the background, loud voices at Beth's end of the phone line.

"I've got to go," she said. "They've come to get us for dinner."

There was a loud chorus of "Merry Christmas" coming from Beth's end.

"We'll let you go," my mother said.

"Enjoy your dinner," my father added.

"Thanks. We will. Merry Christmas, everybody," Beth said.

"Merry Christmas," we all echoed into the phones.

"I'll be waiting at the airport. I love you all."

"And we love you," my mother said.

"We love you," my father repeated. "We'll see you next week."

"Bye-bye, Beth," I said. "And wish Tadpole a merry Christmas, too."

"Bye, Sam. Bye, Mom and Dad."

After we'd all hung up, I wandered to my parents' room. My mother was crying and my father had an arm around her shoulders.

"She's okay," I said. "She's fine."

"I know," my mother blubbered. "It's just . . . just . . . you won't understand until your children grow up and leave home."

"First off, who knows if I'm even going to have children. And second, maybe I'm never going to leave home myself."

"Promise?" she asked.

I jumped onto their bed. "I promise. But you might regret it. Someday you might want me to move to the other side of the country."

She wrapped an arm around me. "Never."

CHAPTER FIVE

—

It had taken me a long time to get back to sleep after Beth's call. Partly that had to do with being woken up in the middle of the night, but partly it was because, as far as my body was concerned, it wasn't really the middle of the night, it was early evening. I always found the time change a bit difficult to adjust to. And as soon as I got myself oriented to local time, it would be time to go back home and start the whole thing over again. That was one of the disadvantages of coming this far for such a short break—but a short holiday was better than no holiday at all. I was going to come here every year, forever. Even when I was married and when I had kids and they had kids and—I was getting a little ahead of myself. Maybe I should wait until I got kissed for the first time before I started planning my wedding!

W
A
V
E

I made my way down to the beach and looked around. It was still early in the day, before the midday sun would drive us all to shelter and shade, so there was a crowd. There were the older, grandparent types, young couples walking hand in hand, and families with little kids—I didn't see any potential brides to propose to.

Sometimes when I looked at a girl I didn't just think about who she was and whether she was cute, I thought about what was inside of her. And I don't mean what sort of person she was, but what was *really* inside, in her genetic code. What was hidden deep beneath the surface in her DNA? Things that you couldn't tell by looking, things that she didn't even know were inside of her but which might change her life, and the life of anybody who was married to her.

MS—Multiple Sclerosis—was somewhere in my mother's genetic programming. Luckily for me, though it was genetic, it wasn't inherited. She didn't get it from her parents. That meant that neither Beth nor I was any more likely to have it than anybody else. We didn't carry that DNA time-bomb inside of us. Not that we couldn't have something else. Who knew what diseases or conditions anybody carried? It was just a gamble. And marriage itself was such a gamble—half of my friends had divorced parents. It made the whole marriage thing look like a real long shot.

I knew that all of this was kind of strange to think about, especially for a twelve-year-old, but maybe it wasn't. I lived with my mother's MS. Even when it went into remission, it was still like living on the side of a volcano. You knew another eruption might be coming at any time, you just didn't know when or how bad it would be.

I sometimes wondered, if my father had known about the MS, would he still have married my mother? I looked over at the two of them sitting side by side in lounge chairs, holding hands. I guess I knew the answer.

My mother wasn't doing so well today. She'd dropped a fork and almost knocked over her juice glass at breakfast this morning, and I was positive that one leg was dragging a bit when she came down to the beach—although everybody looked awkward walking through the sand so maybe I was just imagining it. And even if she was having a harder time today, that was at least partly because of the disturbed sleep. I played it back and forth, feeling anxious and then finding an excuse to explain why I shouldn't be worried. If she was in relapse, then this one was lasting longer than the last . . . but she'd had longer ones before. This relapse would, sooner or later, end in remission like the rest. I hoped.

"Look, there's the beach elephant!" my father said. Sure enough, up the beach was the small elephant that gave rides to kids. "Hey, buddy, you want to go for a little spin, like in the old days?" he asked.

"I think I'll pass on that."

"Are you sure?" my mother asked. "You used to love riding that elephant."

"I also used to be six years old."

"Didn't you ride it last year?" my father asked.

"Two years ago."

"Oh, that long ago . . . back when you were a kid."

"Better a kid than an old man," I joked.

"Are you going to let your son talk to me that way?" my father asked my mother.

"Why is he always *my* son when he does something wrong?" she asked in a mock-hurt tone.

"I think that's obvious."

"Well, even if you don't want to ride it, I'd like to go and see the elephant," my mom said.

She started to get up but seemed to lose her balance and began to tumble backwards. I reached out and offered her a hand to steady her, and my father practically jumped to his feet to help.

"I guess I'm a little unsteady on my feet. How about if my two handsome men escort me over to see the elephant?"

She offered her arms and my father and I took our places on either side of her. Slowly the three of us started across the sand.

"It's another perfect day in Paradise," my mother said.

"That it is," my father agreed.

The weather was what people talked about when they didn't want to talk about anything else. She wasn't doing very well today. That wasn't just my imagination.

"I was thinking that after lunch I might go and have a nap. That call last night was wonderful, but it disturbed my beauty sleep," my mother said.

"And yet I was thinking you looked particularly beautiful this morning!" my father told her.

"Maybe you need a nap too, because clearly your eyes are going," my mother joked. "Although I was hoping that while I was sleeping the two of you would go out and do something fun."

"We could do that. Sam, what do you think would be fun?"

"Snorkeling would be fun."

"Then snorkeling it is. I'll talk to Philippe and ask him to arrange it right after lunch."

We stood among a group of young people waiting and watching while the elephant made its little circuit. I knew the route pretty well—along the beach, up toward the lobby, cutting across the lawn, and back down here to the set of steps used to climb on. While there was no way I was going to ride it, it did bring back some good memories.

I even understood why all these little kids and first-time tourists were so excited. After all, it *was* an elephant. For most kids, the closest they'd ever come to riding any type of animal was one of those fake horses at the grocery store, where your parents would put in fifty cents and the horse would shake and bounce for two minutes.

The mahout led the elephant with a rope attached to a collar around its neck. It reminded me of those pony rides they sometimes had at petting zoos, where a handler led you and the pony around in a little circle. Here it was just a bigger animal and a bigger circle.

Three little kids and their dad were up in the howdah on the elephant's back. They looked as though they were having a good time, laughing and smiling. A woman—I assumed she was the mother—was trotting along, taking pictures.

"The elephant doesn't seem to want to cooperate," my father said.

The mahout was struggling to convince his elephant to come back onto the sand and stay off the grass at the edge of the resort. The elephant was digging in its heels, and it was only with a lot of pulling and encouragement that it started off again.

"Probably doesn't like the hot sand under its feet," my mother suggested.

She was wearing sandals. I was barefoot. The sand wasn't really that hot because it was still pretty early, just before ten.

The elephant sidled up to where we were all standing and nestled against the steps. The father assisted his children down, one by one, with the mahout and the mother helping. Then the father climbed down himself.

Everybody crowded around the elephant. It seemed like a nice animal, very calm and gentle. It reminded me of an old, tame, good-natured horse. Even if you weren't taking a ride, the mahout would let you go up and touch it or give it some fruit from the salad bar. It was probably the best-fed elephant in all of Thailand. I wished I'd thought to grab something.

I also really liked the way the elephant and his

mahout got along. The man was always scratching his elephant behind the ears and talking to it. He said the elephant was trilingual and understood Thai, English, and Swedish. I wasn't so sure about that, but I did know that he never worked it during the heat of midday, and he always gave it buckets and buckets of water.

The next customer, a little girl of seven or eight, walked up the steps and was helped onto the elephant's back by her mother. The mahout made sure she was safely inside the basket and started walking. The elephant followed. Whatever had been bothering it coming down to the steps didn't seem to be bothering it anymore.

"Not much of a life," my mother observed. "Going around and around and getting nowhere."

"Are you talking about being an elephant or being a lawyer?" my father asked.

"At least no one is on your back."

"You obviously haven't been to my office lately," he joked. "Let's go back and arrange the snorkeling. Then I can *swim* in circles."

We left the little group and started back. The elephant was walking ahead of us in the same direction, the little girl on its back, and the girl's mother was walking right beside it. She wasn't taking pictures. She looked nervous, as though she was worrying about being close enough to catch the little girl if she fell. It would have been easier if she'd simply climbed up on the elephant *with* her daughter.

The mahout led the elephant up the beach and away from the ocean. It seemed to be picking up speed, and both the mother and the mahout started to trot faster, as well, to keep pace. It really did seem as though it didn't like the sand and was looking forward to having grass under its feet. It reached the edge of the manicured lawn, but as the mahout turned to complete the circuit the elephant kept going straight ahead! The mahout was almost jerked off his feet but he kept hold of the rope, and the elephant pulled him along. The mahout started yelling at the elephant, digging in his heels to try to stop it. The elephant ignored his voice and his muscle. It kept moving up the grass, dragging him along, toward the resort and away from the beach.

The mother suddenly became aware that things weren't going as they were supposed to and she began to yell and scream, which caused the little girl to start crying. The elephant kept moving—not running, just walking quickly.

"Should we do something?" I asked.

"I don't know if there's anything we can do," my father said. "Look, he's getting some help!"

Two of the resort staff had joined the mahout, one grabbing onto the rope as well and the second trying to block the elephant. The elephant simply brushed past him and continued to drag the other two along.

"Please, both of you, go and see if you can help!" my mother said.

We hesitated for a split second and then we both started running. I wasn't sure what either of us was supposed to do but I *did* want to see what was happening up close.

The elephant loped past the pool, and the whole procession—mahout, mother, and two resort staff—were like a little parade for the people in the lounge chairs. Nimbly the animal negotiated between the people and the chairs. For a split second I thought it was aiming for the salad bar beside the pool, but it bypassed that as well. It kept moving. It wasn't running, just moving at that same steady, quick walk, and we were gaining.

It was headed straight for the door to the lobby, but it made a quick right instead and trotted along the back of the hotel and then up the side, out of sight. We ran faster and rounded the corner as well.

It looked as though the elephant might be slowing down. We kept running, closing the gap quickly. Finally, halfway up the hotel lawn, in the shade of a tree, the elephant came to a stop. The mahout held the elephant in place and my father and I rushed up to help. One of the resort staff grabbed the little girl, lifted her down, and handed her over to her mother. The girl seemed upset, but she started to really cry only when her mother began to wail.

The mahout and the resort staff were yelling at one another in Thai. The mahout then began speaking to the mother, trying to explain and apologize. She seemed too upset to listen. He tried to give her back her money, but she pushed his hand away. Instead, she started to yell at him, which caused her daughter to cry even louder.

I felt sorry for everybody, but especially the elephant. I hoped it wouldn't be punished for what it did. It just didn't want to be on the beach. It wanted to be on the grass in the shade. My father—as always was trying to calm everybody down, and it seemed to be working.

"The important thing is that she's fine," he said to the mother. "How about if you two go inside, and I'm sure the resort will provide the biggest ice cream sundae in the world—free, right?"

The two staff members nodded their heads enthusiastically.

My father dropped to one knee. "What's your name?" he asked the girl.

"Sophie."

"Would you like some ice cream, Sophie?"

She wiped away some tears with the back of her hand and nodded.

"And I'm sure they'll get you a sundae as well," my father suggested, looking up at the woman.

"Forget the ice cream," she said. "I'd like something a little stronger."

"I'm sure that could be arranged." He turned to the staff. "Right?"

The two of them practically tripped over each other offering to help, and then they led the woman and her daughter away and into the hotel lobby.

"Thank you, sir, thank you," the mahout said, as he pumped my father's hand. "I do not know what happened. She is a good elephant . . . never before did she do such a thing . . . you must believe me!"

"We know. We've been coming here for years. My children have been on your elephant before, many times. It was just one of those things."

We started to head back to where Mom was waiting,

and as we walked I could hear the mahout talking to his elephant. He didn't sound angry, just concerned, like a parent.

"Now don't you wish you had gone on the ride when you had the chance?" my father asked.

"That was certainly more exciting than I remember it. Instead of the two of us going snorkeling, do you think Mom might be keen on another elephant ride this afternoon?"

"I think she's going to take it easy for the rest of the day. She's pretty tired."

Tired. That was the word he used when her condition wasn't good.

"Looks like the elephant generated a lot of interest," my father said as we rounded the corner of the building.

Sure enough, a lot of the people who had been lounging by the pool or drinking on the patio were now on their feet, looking at something . . . but they were all staring out, away from the building and toward the beach and the ocean.

"What are they looking at?" I asked.

"Maybe a whale or a shark is near the shore."

I hated sharks, and I'd long ago convinced myself that the water was way too shallow to allow a shark to come close.

We rounded the pool and peered out toward the ocean. I didn't see anything except beach . . . lots and lots of beach. It was as if the ocean had receded.

"I've never seen it like this before," my father said. "The beach has to be a hundred yards wide . . . or wider."

W
A
V
E

Mom had walked up off the beach and was now standing by the pool among a group of people, and she waved at us. We trotted over.

"It just happened," she said, before we could even ask. "It was like the water was just sucked away."

There was a clear line showing where the water level had been. Above that was dry, white sand. On the other side of that line the ocean bottom was exposed. It was hardened, rippled, wet ground, with lots and lots of puddles, little pockets of water left behind when the ocean ran away.

A man ran out onto the newly exposed ocean floor. He picked something up and turned around, holding it up to show us. In his hand was a large fish, still alive, flapping and flopping! It had been left behind when the water retreated. Then I noticed that there were other fish—dozens and dozens of them—tossing and turning in the mud.

"Look at the boats," I said. Farther out there were boats stranded, sitting on the mud at the bottom. A few minutes earlier they'd been bobbing on the waves.

"What could have caused this?" my father asked.

"Perhaps it's like an extra-low tide," a man standing beside us suggested.

My father shook his head. "No, that's not right. High tide was at nine this morning. This is pretty much high tide."

"Looks pretty low to me," the man said. He had a strong German accent.

"Even if it were low tide, it's never like this," my father replied.

"It is now. Some places in the world have gigantic tide changes," the man said. "I have heard of such places."

"Yes, but this isn't one of them. The slope is shallow, so high and low tides have a difference of only twenty or thirty yards here. I've been coming here for years and I've never seen anything like this." My father turned to one of the resort staff who had come out to look. "Have *you* ever seen anything like this before?"

He just shook his head. He was staring, open-mouthed, looking perfectly stunned. I looked from face to face. That was the expression on most people. Others just looked amused.

More and more people came out of the resort—guests and staff alike—and stood watching. As a group we moved closer to the water; it was almost magnetic.

"Great chance to walk on the bottom of the ocean," somebody said. "Let's go."

I'd started to walk along with them when my father put a hand on my shoulder. "Let's just stay here."

"Why?"

"I don't know. Let's just stay."

I was going to say something when I realized his reluctance probably had more to do with my mother than anything else, so I didn't argue.

"If he wants to go out, if you both want to go out, I'll just wait here," my mother said. Apparently she was thinking the same thing.

"No," my father replied. "Let's watch for a minute . . . this doesn't seem right . . . the ocean doesn't just run away for no reason. And it's still going out."

He was right. The open ocean bottom was becoming wider and wider. It was so strange.

"What do you think is happening?" I asked.

He just shook his head.

While some people stayed on the patio with us, a whole lot of others were going down to the beach and out to the ocean floor. They skipped around the puddles, picking up or nudging the fish that lay gasping there. I couldn't help but wonder how fast the water had been traveling if even fish couldn't keep up.

All along the beach, as far as I could see in both directions, people were out, standing, watching, or even walking toward the water's edge. It had to be two hundred yards away now . . . maybe farther. And was the water still receding? How far could it possibly go?

"What's that sound?" my mother asked.

I pricked up my ears. I couldn't hear anything . . . maybe it was the wind. That would make sense—maybe the wind had blown the water out—but I didn't even feel a breeze.

"Oh my God," my father gasped. "It's the water . . . it's coming back in, and it's coming in fast!"

CHAPTER SIX

—

We stood there and watched as a wave of water rushed forward, reclaiming the bottom of the ocean. It was impossible to tell how big it was until it reached the first people—they were knocked over, submerged, and disappeared under the racing wave! People walking on the ocean bottom and on the beach began to run, but it was as if they were standing still or running in place as the wave just overwhelmed them and they were lost beneath the water!

"We have to run!" my father yelled.

"But we're well away from the—"

My father grabbed my mother by the arm, cutting her off. "Just *run!*"

I grabbed her other arm and we started moving as quickly as she could manage toward the hotel. Other people, able to move more rapidly, raced past us, pushing the lounge chairs out of the way as they went. Others just stood there watching, and a few people were still staring out, standing there, or even walking toward the water. How dangerous could it be if people were walking toward it?

I looked over my shoulder and felt a rush of adrenaline as I realized that the wave was getting bigger and bigger and coming closer and closer! It had already filled in the entire ocean again and now it was racing up the beach! It was moving so fast that there was no way we would get to the building before it reached us! I had to fight the urge to just let go of my mother's arm and run. I held tight, trying to help her move faster.

"We're not going to make it!" I screamed.

"Keep running!"

I could hear the wave rushing up behind us and the roar was punctuated by the sounds of people screaming and yelling.

We were getting closer and closer to the hotel and safety—and then, I was knocked off my feet!

For a split second I was under the water, and then I broke the surface, surfing along on the wave as it raced toward the hotel. I braced myself as I hit the building and bounced backwards! I tried to stand up but I was hit by a wall of water and went underneath the surface again and was spun around. Then something pulled me to the surface. It was my father. He had my arm in a firm grip and he dragged me forward, banging me against something, until finally I thumped up onto a set of stairs. He kept pulling me up and I struggled to my feet.

I looked up. My mother was a few steps above me.

"Keep climbing! Don't stop!" my father yelled.

I ran to my mother and took her hand and we scrambled up to the first landing of the open-air staircase as the water washed up the stairs behind us.

"Don't stop!"

We made the turn and at last got to the second story.

"We'll be safe here," my father said.

We looked over the edge. What I saw was unbelievable. The whole patio, the whole pool area was under water! It was like watching a raging, racing river, white water slamming up against everything. Caught in its grip were lounge chairs and branches and the salad bar and *people*! Some people were being tossed around like rag dolls, while others were clinging to trees. Two men were standing on the top of the diving tower, surrounded by water.

The air was filled with the sound of shrieking and hollering, objects smashing, wood splintering and snapping, and then there was an explosion, and the crash of breaking glass!

"It's taken out the windows in the lobby!" my father exclaimed.

"All those people down there in the water! We have to help, we have to do something!" my mother screamed.

"I don't know what we can do . . . maybe I can reach somebody down below . . . you two stay here . . . unless you need to climb higher."

He started back down the stairs. I could see that the first landing was still just above water, but I couldn't see around the corner as he disappeared. I couldn't just stand there, not knowing. I broke free of my mother's hand and ran down the stairs.

"Sam!" she screamed.

I ignored her and jumped down to the landing. My father was just below, half in the water, reaching down to help a woman still caught in the current. Her head was all bashed and bleeding. He pulled her up and out.

"Let me help," I said.

He looked surprised to see me, but then nodded his approval. "Bring her up to your mother."

I didn't want to leave him but there really wasn't much choice. I took the woman he'd rescued by the hand. She looked dazed, her eyes glazed over and staring straight ahead. She didn't even acknowledge me as I led her up the stairs. We had gone only a few steps when we reached my mother, who was coming down, looking for me. Before she had a chance to yell at me she saw the woman and offered her a hand.

"You come up with us," she said to me.

I shook my head. "I'm fine. Dad's below. He might need my help."

She looked as though she was going to argue or object, but she didn't.

"Be careful!"

As she started up the stairs, I went back down. My father was now almost completely under water. He was still standing on the stairs. The way the stairwell was aimed, the force of the water, the wave, the current, couldn't pull him out. I went down a few steps, stopping when the water was just above my waist.

My father turned around and saw me. I thought he was going to order me back. I didn't want to go back.

"Keep your hand on the railing—it's solid—and come down farther."

That wasn't what I'd expected. I didn't know whether I was happy or not. I did know I was scared.

I went down one more step, and then another.

"The water has slowed down," my father said.

"It's still the same height, though. It hasn't fallen."

"Not fallen. Not rising. It's an ocean now, not a river. I think I'm okay to go out there."

"You can't do that!" I screamed.

"No choice. I don't think they can hold on much longer." He pointed.

There was a woman holding a small child—more like a baby, a year or so old—clinging to a tree with her free hand.

"I'm coming!" my father yelled out to her, and she looked over at us with pleading, terrified eyes.

"There's hardly any current at all now," he said.

I was scared, but if anybody could do it, it was my father.

He let himself go and swam toward her. There was a wooden chair—a chair from the lobby—spinning toward him. He bumped into the chair, pushed it out of the way, and then swam to the woman. She let go of the tree and wrapped her one arm desperately around his neck. She was struggling, clawing at him, and for a second she pushed his head beneath the surface. He popped back up and I could see him talking to her, trying to calm her. She settled down then and stopped struggling and grabbed the tree again.

She released her baby into his left arm and then put both her arms around the tree. Was it my imagination or was that tree tilting over to one side?

With the baby tucked under one arm my father began to side-stroke toward the stairwell. At first it looked as though he wasn't moving, but he slowly came closer and closer. I reached out as far as I could and plucked the baby from his arm. Its eyes were wide open, a look of terror on its face. It didn't struggle or cry as it was handed from one stranger to another.

"Bring the baby up to your mother. I'm going back for the mom."

I sloshed up the stairs, keeping one hand on the railing and my other arm tightly wrapped around the kid. I didn't want to trip, but more importantly, I didn't want to drop the baby. We hit the landing—wasn't that above the water level before?—and turned up the steps to the second level. The second step up was above water.

"Mom!" I yelled as I reached the top. She was on her knees beside the woman we'd already rescued. She was holding a cloth, a pool towel, against the cut on the side of the woman's head. It was stained with blood.

"A baby? But where is its—?"

"Dad's gone back for the mother. Here."

She took the baby and I raced back down. Hitting the water on the landing, I looked over the railing. I was in time to see Dad and the woman together, holding onto the tree. Why was he still out there? Why hadn't he come back?

"Dad!" I yelled.

He looked up at me. "She's afraid to let go . . . to let go of the tree!" he yelled back, his voice barely audible over the roar of the water and the sound of smashing and crashing—and screaming.

In the background a whole chorus of voices, calling out names, pleaded for help. Most of the words I couldn't understand. They probably weren't even English.

The water continued to rush past my father. It was filled with debris—pieces of wood and broken hotel furniture. As it raced by, some of it crashed against the tree and some narrowly missed my father. He was in danger. I knew he wouldn't leave that women, but he couldn't very well force her to come. And I was there, watching, helpless. If only I could throw him a rope. But where was I going to get a rope . . . or something like a rope? A fire hose! I could throw him a fire hose!

I raced back up the stairs to the second floor. I looked down the hall toward my mother and then in the other direction before I saw it, a box sticking out of the wall. I threw open the front. The hose inside was all tightly coiled. I grabbed the nozzle and started running while the hose spun out behind me with a whirring sound. I splashed down the stairs again, struggling as the water got deeper and deeper. I stopped before the water rose past my chest. I pulled the hose, hand over hand, getting more and more slack. I needed at least thirty feet of hose to get it that far. It kept coming and coming and then it thumped to a stop. Did I have enough? And even if I did, could I throw it that far? Or did I need to throw it at all?

Carefully I took the hose and looped it around my waist. I threaded the nozzle back through and tied a knot. I gave it a pull to check the knot. It was solid. I reached over and pulled the other end. It was solidly attached up at the tap on the second floor. I could swim out and there would be no danger of me being dragged away by the current. I was anchored to this lifeline.

I moved farther down the steps until the water was so deep that my choices were to go no farther, go under water, or start swimming. I took a deep breath and dove in. I pushed myself along the wall—the water was almost as high as the ceiling now. I had a rush of fear, of second thoughts. No time for that. If the water was still rising, it had to happen now.

I pushed off, away from the stairwell and into the open water. The current grabbed me and I struggled against it. My father was just up ahead. I could see him and the woman clinging to the tree, but they were looking the other way and he hadn't noticed me. I started swimming as hard as I could. I was in the current's grip but I was making progress. I was getting closer and closer—and a lounge chair came streaking toward me! I didn't have time to get out of its way, but I put up my hand and deflected it to the side.

I was pushed farther away. For an instant I thought about just quitting, letting the current push me back and then pulling myself up the stairs. I could still do that if I had to, but I didn't have to yet. They were so close. I dug in with my arms and kicked my feet with all my strength. I was just a few feet away.

"Dad!" I screamed.

He turned around. His eyes opened in shock and fear. He reached out and grabbed my arm and pulled me over to the tree.

"What are you doing!" he yelled.

"I came to help."

"The best way you could have helped was to . . . what's around your . . . a fire hose?"

"I couldn't find a rope so—"

"Here, let me have it. Hold on to the tree, wrap both arms around it."

It was just a small palm tree, and I was practically on top of the woman. She had that same glazed look that her baby had. Her eyes were wide open but she was staring at nothing. Despite the warmth of the air and water she was shaking violently.

My father took the hose off my waist and tied it around the woman, making sure the knot was tight.

"We're going to swim back," he told me. "Me and you."

"But what about her?"

"She's staying here for a minute."

"But you can't just leave her!"

"I'm not leaving her. Keep one hand on the hose and let the current push you along. Just try to aim for the stairwell. I'll be right beside you."

"But—"

"No time to argue. Now!"

He grabbed me by the arm and practically ripped me off the tree. "You've got a grip on the hose?"

I nodded.

"Then let's go!"

We dove in. The current was fast and we were pushed along. I kept a hand on the hose to guide me, and my father was right there at my side. There was no time for fear. Within seconds we'd hit the stairwell, and I put both hands on the hose, pulling myself up and onto the stairs. My father was right there, pushing me up until we bumped something solid and I was standing.

"Go up a few steps and get ready to pull!" he ordered.

"What?" What was he talking about?

"The hose . . . get ready to pull the hose . . . we're going to pull her off that tree and over here to safety."

"Does she know we're going to do that?"

"She doesn't know anything. She's in shock, and she can't stay there. That tree is about to be washed away."

My father started to pull in the slack on the fire hose. I did the same until we were both holding it, stretched taut across the open water to the woman. I couldn't see her, but I could just imagine what was going to happen, her panic when we'd start to pull her, and her terror when she'd feel herself being dragged through the water.

"Now!" my father yelled.

Hand over hand we started to haul in the fire hose. More and more hose was pulled through our hands, and then at last the woman splashed into view! She was crying and sputtering, and as my father grabbed her she started thrashing her arms and legs and scratching. He spun her around, pinning her arms against her sides, but she started screaming.

"You're safe!" he yelled. "You're safe now!"

She kept screaming and—

"I'll bring you to your baby. He's all right."

She stopped struggling. She stopped screaming.

My father led her up the stairs. The fire hose was still tied around her waist. She stumbled, and I reached out and took her other arm. We reached the second floor and she saw her baby and burst from us, the fire hose trailing behind her as she ran. She scooped the baby from my mother and wrapped her arms around it, clinging to it with all her might.

"You did it," my mother said to my father. "You saved her."

"Not me. Him." He pointed at me. "To come up with an idea like the fire hose under these conditions is nothing short of brilliant." He put an arm around my shoulder. "But if you ever put yourself at risk like that again, I'll personally drown you myself, do you understand?"

"Yes, sir."

He wrapped both arms around me and squeezed me so tightly that I had trouble drawing a breath. He was shaking . . . or was it me? . . . or was it both of us? A third set of arms—my mother's—wrapped around us.

"I need both of you to stay here now," my mother said. "I can't risk losing either of you . . . I was so scared."

"We're okay. Let's take care of the people who are here."

He went over and untied the fire hose from the woman.

"*Danke . . . danke sehr* . . . thank you," she said. "You . . . you saved"—she gestured to her child—"*mein sohn* and me."

"It was nothing," my father said. "We just did what we had to do."

Now that she was sitting there and everything had calmed down, I knew I recognized her. I'd seen her and the baby and her husband on the beach, the little one always under an umbrella, protected from the sun. I knew what her husband, the baby's father, looked like. He was tall and had blond hair and he couldn't have been any older than she was—maybe in his early thirties. I knew they were German and friendly. The only thing that mattered now, though, I didn't know. Where was he?

For the first time I noticed that there were other people in the corridor. Some were dressed and dry while others looked like drowned rats. They had cuts and scrapes and—I looked at my own arm and saw that it was all scraped. I just hadn't noticed. It didn't bother me but it looked ugly, looked like it should be hurting. Great, something to look forward to.

My father walked over to the railing and I followed. Below was an ocean of water. The patio, the beach, the pool were all under water, all gone, disappeared, as if they'd never been there at all. The tree where the woman had been clinging—where we'd been clinging—was gone. Almost all of the trees and bushes that had provided shade for the pool were either under water or washed away completely. For the first time I looked up from the water and to the hotel itself. There were dozens and dozens of people standing on balconies, looking down. Some of them had cameras or video recorders. I wondered if what we had done had been captured on tape. Maybe I should have smiled or waved . . . how bizarre. People were still snapping pictures.

In the background, voices were still calling out. Some sounded almost calm, others were pleading, desperate. I scanned the area, looking for the people, but I couldn't see anything but water and debris and . . . the water and the objects floating on the surface were no longer being swept inland. Everything was now being pulled back toward the ocean again. The water was rushing out and, judging by the speed of the objects on the surface, it was moving almost as fast as it had before, but now in the opposite direction.

I stood there, watching, trying to figure out if what I thought was happening was really happening. If the water was flowing back, if it was being sucked back toward the ocean, then that meant it was all over, that we were safe . . . didn't it?

"Look!" my father yelled, and he pointed.

There, almost directly below us, was a man in the water. He had one arm wrapped around a log and he was waving with the other. He and the log were being pulled out.

"Catch!" my father screamed.

Now I understood why he had dragged the fire hose over with him. He threw it and it sailed into the air. The man desperately reached for it but it flew too far, over his head. But that was okay . . . the log was headed right for the hose! He could still get it.

The man leaped into the water and grabbed the fire hose, and it almost instantly went taut as the current tried to pull him farther away. For a second my mind raced— was this the baby's father? No, this man was older, bigger, and his hair was gray.

My father held tight and I grabbed on as well. We started pulling on the fire hose, reeling the man in like a big fish! We struggled, frantically, foot by foot, moving him closer. He was bigger than the woman, and now the current was pulling away from where we were instead of helping us. We were making progress, straining, fighting against the current, but it was so slow and—I tumbled backwards, and my father landed on top of me! The fire hose was still in our hands but it was obvious that there was no longer anything on the other end.

My father jumped to his feet and ran for the railing. I scrambled after him and got there in time to see the man flailing and pawing at the water. Then he disappeared beneath the surface. He just had to get back to the surface and grab onto something else. There was so much floating around for him to hold on to. I waited and waited, watching and . . . nothing. The debris that had surrounded him bobbed and swirled and then it all disappeared into the distance. And I knew he wasn't coming back up.

CHAPTER SEVEN

—

It took longer for the water to flow out than it had to rush in, but now it was almost all gone. My father and mother and I waded through the knee-deep water that remained. The whole patio—including chairs, tables, trees, bushes, and shrubs—had been scoured clean. All that remained was the deck itself and the pool, which was a filthy brown, practically filled in by the sand that had been carried up by the wave and left behind as the water receded. The water was still flowing back out to the sea, but it was now so low and moving so gently that it was no longer capable of carrying anything with it.

Everywhere there was garbage—clothing, merchandise from the shops on the road, lamps, garbage cans, pieces of wood, fallen palm trees, bicycles, motor scooters, and even a big refrigerator. I had an urge to open its door and see if I could find a cool drink.

The debris, the destruction, that was bad. Other things were tragic. There were people yelling out names, asking each person they passed if he or she had seen the loved one they couldn't find. Maybe they'd been torn away from each other when the wave hit. I didn't even want to think about it. Maybe one of them was looking for that man who had been swept away. How many people were missing—or dead?

"Be careful of the glass," my father said as he led us into the lobby through the opening where the full-length picture windows had once been. The water was almost gone but the carpets were sopping wet, and there was more garbage and sand . . . and a taxicab, on its side, was pinned against the front desk! I pointed at it, in awe.

"Quite the parking spot," my father said.

I snorted, and then felt bad. The last thing I'd expected was a joke. He smiled at me.

"How did it even get in here?" I asked.

He gestured to the front doors leading to the street. They were ripped off the hinges. It must have been sitting up front and been pulled in when the water receded.

The little bit of furniture that remained was all pushed against the walls and had been smashed and overturned. Without the furniture, people were sitting on the floor. Some of them were in tears. Some were yelling, angrily, and others, even stranger, were laughing. There were also those who were sitting silently, staring blankly, in shock.

Some people were hovering, while others were racing around. The staff, usually so calm, were almost frantic.

My mother bent down beside a woman who was quietly sobbing. She was holding her arm.

"Let me have a look," she said.

The woman hesitated.

"It's okay, I'm a nurse."

The woman raised her arm and my mother carefully examined it, asking questions.

It was strange to see her this way. She was my mom, not a nurse. And it had been six or seven years since she'd even worked as a nurse . . . since about the time the MS first hit.

"It's definitely broken. I'm going to immobilize it and then we'll get a doctor to set it and you'll be okay. Don't worry." My mother stood up and turned to us. "I'm going to stay here and help sort out the injuries."

"We're going to look around," my father said. "Check things out more thoroughly."

We moved through the lobby and out the front door. The driveway and the road behind that were devoid of traffic. No cars or taxis or even bicycles. There were people wandering about, picking up the remains of the little kiosks. The tourists looked stunned. They were wandering, bumping into one another, aimless, as though they couldn't believe any of this. How could they? I certainly didn't.

The roads were wet and there were puddles and mud to show where the ocean had been. It might just as easily have been a heavy rain instead of a flood. Then I saw a couple of fish flapping on the ground. Only a flood could leave fish behind.

Lumbering up the road through the crowd was an elephant—the elephant from the beach. The mahout was at its side. I hadn't even thought about what might have happened to them, but obviously they were fine. We walked up to meet them.

"I'm glad to see you're both okay," my father said.

"Because of my elephant," he said. "She knew. That is why she would not stay on the beach . . . she knew."

"I've heard about animals sensing things," my father said.

"She felt it," the mahout said. "In her feet, or maybe she heard it, but she knew. The girl . . . the one when she ran away . . . have you seen her and her mother?"

"I saw them in the lobby," my father said. "They're fine. And for that, they should be grateful to your elephant."

The mahout looked confused.

"If your elephant hadn't taken them away on that extra little ride, they would still have been down on the beach. They could have died. Your elephant might have saved their lives."

"I had not thought of that. She saved my life, as well," the mahout said.

"I guess she did," my father agreed.

"And ours," I said.

My father looked at me intently, as though he was trying to understand what I meant.

"We were on the beach too. We came up to help, and then Mom followed us. There's no way we could have made it to the stairwell—for sure no way *she* could have made it— if we'd been right down on the beach when the wave came."

Slowly my father nodded in agreement. He held out his hand and shook the mahout's. "Thank you."

"You are most welcome, sir."

"And thank you," my father said as he patted the elephant's flank. He turned back to the mahout. "I want to give you something as thanks." He dug into his pocket and turned it inside out. It was empty. "I'm sorry, my money is gone . . . it's been washed away. Tomorrow I'll give you something."

"That is not necessary, sir."

"But I want to do that. Tomorrow, promise you'll come and see me. We're in bungalow number . . ." He stopped. "The bungalow is right on the beach. I don't know what happened to our things. We have to look."

He rushed off and I stumbled after him. He turned back around. "Tomorrow, come and see me!" he yelled.

We hurried along the side of the hotel. The tree where the elephant had stopped was ripped almost out of the ground. Grass and trees and the ornamental rockery were all swept away.

By now the water level had dropped even more, so that we were just sloshing around in ankle-deep water as we crossed the pool deck. Some of the dunes on the beach had broken above the surface again. I looked down at the closest bungalow. The back window was blown out and there was some debris on the roof—the water had been that high. Our bungalow was no bigger or higher or farther from the ocean than that one. Whatever we had was going to be gone or ruined. I'd hardly gotten a chance to listen to my iPod, and that really didn't seem fair . . . I stopped myself. I was worrying about my iPod and other people were looking for family members. Stupid, stupid, stupid. How could I even think about that when people had lost their lives?

"Hey!" a voice called out.

We turned around to see a man jogging toward us.

"You do not know me," he said in a thick accent.

I didn't know him, but I knew who he was.

"My name is Hans. It was my wife and baby who were in the tree." His English was excellent but there was an unmistakable German accent.

"Oh, of course!" my father said. "I've seen you around the compound. In all the confusion I didn't recognize you. I just couldn't put it together."

"I was not here," Hans said. "I was up on the street."

That would explain why his clothes were dry. He hadn't gone through the flood.

"When I heard, I raced back—I was not far—and then to find my wife and son . . ." He started to cry.

"How are they doing?" my father asked.

"Fine. Good. Scared, but alive . . . because of you two. My wife told me everything."

I wondered how he felt about us yanking her out of the tree against her will.

"You saved them."

"They might have been fine without us," my father said.

"She told me the tree was washed away, that she would have drowned."

"We just did what had to be done. If it hadn't been us it would have been somebody else."

"But it was not somebody else. It was you and your son."

He threw his arms around my father and hugged him and then did the same with me.

"If ever I can help . . . I do not know how such a thing could be repaid."

"I'm just glad we could be there. Your thank-you is more than enough," my father said.

"No, no," he said, shaking his head vigorously. "Here, you must take this." He held out a card. "This is my name and my company. You must call, you must come to Germany as my guest."

"That's very generous, but you don't have to—"

"No, I insist." He pressed the card into my father's hand. "Please, now I must go back. My wife, I need to take her and my son to see a doctor . . . just to be safe." He paused. "I owe you everything."

He hugged my father and me again and then he hurried off.

"Sort of makes me feel pretty small to be worried about our lost luggage," my father said.

"Or an iPod," I added.

"Those things can all be replaced. I'm just hoping that our passports are still there. It'll all be harder without them."

The entire beach was now above water. We trudged along the deep sand toward our bungalow.

"What do you think caused it?" I asked.

"Something probably happened under water, like a landslide or an earthquake."

"I didn't feel any earthquake."

"It could have happened a long way from here. We probably won't know much until we turn on CNN or—" He stopped and spun around. "Your sister is going to hear about this. We have to get to a phone and call her as soon as possible. What time is it?"

"I think just after ten, maybe ten-thirty."

"No, I mean in New York. If it's eleven hours later here then it's about eleven-thirty, just before midnight. She'll still be up . . . up celebrating Christmas . . . it's still Christmas in New York."

That thought echoed around my head. It was Christmas, but this was no Christmas celebration, no miracle . . . unless you considered us still being alive a miracle.

"Can you imagine how worried she'll be if she hears about this but doesn't know we're safe?"

I could only imagine how she'd feel, how I would feel.

"We have to talk to her before she hears about it on the news," my father said.

"But it won't be reported immediately, will it?" I asked.

"No, even something big like this would take at least a few hours to get reported. We'll call her as soon as we get back up to the lobby."

As soon as he said it, we both knew that wasn't going to work. Even if they did push aside the overturned taxi, the phones would have been ripped out or ruined.

"I'll get a taxi and go inland until I find a phone that works. I'm going to need to find our money, or credit cards, or something. Come on."

We passed by the first bungalow. The windows and front door were all smashed and gone. The roof was wet and a lounge chair was stuck in the palm leaves. My father kept walking, and I stopped and looked inside. The bungalow was a complete disaster. It was almost empty, and the few items of furniture that remained were piled up against the far wall in a tangled mess. I didn't see anything that would show that anybody had been there. There was no clothing, no shoes or personal things littered about. Whatever had been there wasn't there anymore.

Maybe the other bungalows hadn't been hit this hard, maybe ours would be fine. I ran to catch up with my father, who was moving very quickly. Before I reached him he disappeared into our bungalow. I ran through the thick, wet sand, as fast as I could.

I skidded to a stop as I entered. The floor was ankle-deep in sand. There was practically nothing left. The whole room had been scoured of almost every single piece of furniture. The one exception was the TV, smashed and sitting in the corner. My iPod had been sitting on top of the TV. All that remained were the pictures on the wall. They were attached to the wall with screws, and the wave of water couldn't pry them loose. There was no way anything could have survived this. Something powerful enough to take away furniture wasn't going to spare our clothes or papers. It had taken everything.

Then I had a terrible thought. If my mother had gone for that nap she would be dead. We might not even have been able to find her body. She would have been washed out to sea.

My father walked out of his bedroom. "Bingo." He held his wallet and our passports in his hand.

"But how is that possible?"

"They were in the safe in the closet, and the safe is bolted into the floor."

"The safe! I hadn't even thought of that!"

"They're not even wet. Apparently, the safe is waterproof."

I burst into laughter. It wasn't that any of this was funny. I just felt such a wave of relief . . . maybe *wave* wasn't the word I wanted right now.

"Let's get back up. I want you to stay with your mother while I go and look for a phone."

"No!" I said, and realized that I'd practically screamed it. "We all need to stick together."

"We're okay now. There's no need to—"

"No," I said again. "Beth needs to talk to all of us. We all need to be together."

I expected him to argue. He didn't. "You're right. Let's get back up to the lobby and get your mother."

We walked through the front doorway. There was no door to close or lock and nothing inside to worry about anyway. I stopped just outside and stood there in the sand. The two palm trees that had grown beside our bungalow were gone—one was a snapped-off, splintered stub and the second had left no trace, not even a hole in the ground. The flowers were all gone as well. The ocean was still out there, but I didn't know if I could ever look at it in the same way again. Would I ever be able to just sit on the beach, or play in the sand, or wade in the shallows, or . . . the beach . . . oh my God.

"Dad, the beach . . . it's too wide . . . the water is being drawn out again."

He looked out, hard, and then back at me. He looked scared.

"We have to get up to the lobby . . . we have to get farther away."

CHAPTER EIGHT

—

We made our way along the beach as quickly as we could move in the sand. I tried to look back over my shoulder at the ocean as we ran. People had come back down to the beach, and some of them were already down on the exposed ocean bottom again. What was wrong with these people? Had they already forgotten what happened right before the wave hit? Now, instead of picking up fish, they were grabbing articles of clothing or furniture or . . . bodies. There were at least two bodies that I could see. One already had a group of people gathered around it. The other was lying face down in the mud, no more than fifty feet out.

"Hey!" my father yelled at them, startling me. "Get off the beach! Get off the beach!"

A couple of people looked up at him.

"It's still dangerous!" he yelled. "You have to leave!"

Some of them seemed to hear and listen and started to walk away from the water. Others ignored him or didn't seem to understand.

He muttered something under his breath but kept on running. I was afraid that he was going to try to convince them, go down and talk to them, but he didn't. That was reassuring, and frightening. This wasn't just me and my imagination. He thought this was dangerous too. We just had to get up to the hotel. Once we were there we'd be safe, and—I heard the sound at the same instant my father heard it. He looked back. I was afraid to look, but I had to. I turned and saw the massive wave washing across the flats!

"Run!" my father screamed as he grabbed me by the hand.

It was like some sort of nightmare—running from a killer through what felt like quicksand and not being able to move fast enough to escape. We stumbled up onto the pool deck. It was solid underfoot and I could run faster. There were other people running and screaming, and the sound of the water became louder and louder until it overwhelmed everything else. We were almost at the lobby, where my mother was, and I dared to glance over my shoulder again. There was a wall of water racing toward us, towering high over our heads!

We were picked up and I was plunged under the water, twisting and turning and spinning like a sock in some kind of gigantic washing machine! I slammed into something and started to scream but shut my mouth tightly when I realized I was still under water. I tried to look around but couldn't see anything, or even figure out which way was up or over or out. And then my head popped above the surface. I gasped for air, catching a mouthful before I was sucked back down and spun around and around. Things I couldn't see were bashing into my legs, my body, the side of my head. I popped to the surface again, and in that instant realized I was in the lobby, with the roof just inches above my head, being pushed along toward the front doors!

My whole body slammed hard against something and I was spun around as the wave washed me out through those doors. I was part of a river of water that had overwhelmed the entire hotel and was sweeping me up the street. I grasped and grabbed and pushed away from the pieces of debris that filled the water. I was part of an avalanche of objects, bouncing against me and each other and the things that remained standing.

I struggled, trying desperately to fight my way out, going under, kicking to the surface, being smashed and hit and battered and tossed. I grabbed on to a tree, but the force of the water pulled me off and spun me around. I slammed into something—a wall—and the air was forced from my lungs. The water pinned me in place and I reached up, trying to pull myself free, trying to climb the wall, trying to get free of the water. Then something smashed into the back of my head and my whole body burned with pain. I felt myself go limp and my vision got blurry and my legs were suddenly numb. I had to pull myself up just a little . . . just a little . . .

W
A
V
E

BETH

CHAPTER NINE

—

I woke up to a dim winter dawn peeking around my dorm room curtains and opened one eye to look at the clock. It was still just seven-thirty in the morning! Apparently, even when I stayed up late and tried to sleep in, my body still wanted to wake up in time for swim practice. Except I didn't have a practice today, which made it all seem unusually cruel.

I knew from experience that getting back to sleep was now unlikely, but I pulled the blankets up around my ears, closed my eyes again, and tried to think of something pleasant, peaceful . . . like the beach in Thailand, the warm sun, the gently lapping waves . . . the beach where my parents and my little brother were right now, and not me. They'd be swimming in that sparkling ocean water, and all I had to look forward to was an Olympic-sized pool in freezing cold Minnesota.

Sure, it had been my decision to stay home over Christmas—as if the swim coach would have let me make any other decision—but that didn't mean I wasn't jealous of the others. I'd really wanted to pack my bikini and hop on that plane with them, but I had important reasons not to, and they weren't all about swimming. I needed them to know that I was really, truly independent now. I hoped Mom and Dad would get the message that I was okay on my own and they didn't need to worry about me at all. That was important, because Dad had enough on his plate these days with his high-stress job and worrying about Mom.

When her MS symptoms had first started to become obvious, Dad had explained it all to me—what it meant, what we could expect in the days ahead, how we would have to change our lives—in a way that he didn't with Sam. Sam was just a kid, after all. I was pretty sure he didn't think about much except sports and video games, and his idea of planning ahead was trying to figure out what was for dinner. I sure hoped he was doing what I asked and helping out more with Mom, keeping an eye on her for me, letting Dad get a real break.

This was not helping me get back to sleep—and the phone started ringing. I rolled over, grabbed it, and mumbled some sort of hello.

"Beth?"

"Yeah . . . Tad . . . good morning. Isn't this kind of early to be calling? Don't tell me you can't sleep either."

"Sorry, I didn't want to wake you, but I thought I'd better. Have you been watching TV?" he asked.

"It's seventy-thirty in the morning, Tad. I was *sleeping.*"

"You have to turn it on. Something's happened."

I sat up, yawned, and rubbed my eyes. There was always something happening somewhere in the world, and since Tad was hoping to specialize in international law he was always concerned. It was one of the things I loved about him.

"So, what happened?"

"There's been an earthquake just off the coast of Indonesia."

"Indonesia. A big one?"

"Really big. I'm worried about your parents."

"No need to worry, they're in Thailand." How could he get those two confused?

"I know that," he said.

"Yeah, well, the two places are about a thousand miles apart."

"I know that, too. The earthquake was in the ocean off the coast of Indonesia in a place called Banda Aceh. It's fifty miles north of Sumatra."

"It would have to be big to bother Thailand."

"It isn't the quake. It's what it caused. There was a tsunami."

"A tsunami . . . you mean, like a tidal wave?"

"It hit Indonesia and Malaysia and Sri Lanka . . . and Thailand. Just put on the TV. Really. Just do it, *please.*"

There was something about his voice, like he was pleading, or begging—or scared. That wasn't like Tad at all.

"There have been deaths . . . a lot of deaths. Please put on the TV."

"Okay. I'll call you back when—"

"No!" he snapped, and I nearly jumped out of my skin. "I'll stay on the phone," he said. His voice was back to being calm, but that didn't make me feel any more relaxed.

I jumped out of bed, holding the phone by my side, and looked for the remote. Where had it gone? I started to search and—never mind, I didn't need the remote to turn in on. I reached over and clicked the power button. MTV was on, the station I'd been watching when I turned it off last night.

"What channel?"

"Lots of them. CNN or any of the news channels."

Lots . . . that wasn't good. I pushed the "up" button and the TV started to surf through the channels. As it was heading up the dial for CNN, I caught a glimpse of something. I stopped and started back the other way. There it was.

The scene showed a wave quickly rising up and over a cement seawall, and then shooting over, racing up a beach and into some houses. There was screaming and yelling and the sound of objects smashing, and then people overwhelmed by the wave, caught up, spun around, finally vanishing beneath the water. It was awful, just awful! Those poor people!

The images changed. An unseen speaker yelled, "Get inside! Get inside!" and then a wall of water practically engulfed the photographer, and the image died. Next there was a bus lying on its side in the water, spinning, almost completely submerged. People were clinging to it, standing on the top, as all around them flowed a river of scraps and garbage.

The image was replaced by that of an anchorman, sitting at a desk. Behind him was a large graphic, a map of the area.

"Those images, shot by tourists on vacation," he said, "document the terrible tragedy that unfolded. This catastrophe began when an underwater earthquake, fifty miles north of Sumatra and five and a half miles below the surface, struck at 7:58 a.m., local time. This quake was one of the most powerful ever recorded and registered 9.3 on the Richter scale."

On the map a little symbol, showing where the earthquake took place, was added. It was in the ocean, close to Indonesia, pretty far away from Thailand. But I could see the island of Phuket, where my family was, on the map . . . it was far south, as close to the quake as any part of Thailand could be.

"Within twenty minutes, the first of three waves rocked the coast of Sumatra. This wave was believed to be over forty feet tall, while the third wave was reported to be more than twice that height."

A series of little red ripples radiated out from the earthquake site and hit against the coast of Indonesia.

"The tsunami was traveling at speeds of close to five hundred miles per hour across the open ocean. This is comparable to the speed of a jet airplane," the announcer continued. "At approximately 9:45, the first of a series of waves hit Thailand."

The red ripples hit the coast of Thailand and the word "Phuket" flashed on the screen. I dropped the phone and it hit the floor with a loud thud.

"Thousands of people, having just finished breakfast, were caught off guard."

I thought back to talking to my parents on the phone. I tried to do a quick calculation. That must have been before the wave hit, but when, how much earlier? Did it matter?

"At 11:30 a.m., local time, the first wave hit the island country of Sri Lanka and the southern and eastern coasts of India."

The little red ripples got bigger and bigger until they made contact with India and Sri Lanka.

"This was almost four hours from the time of the earthquake, over two hours after the devastation of Thailand and three hours after the tsunami first hit Sumatra. Yet, unbelievably, in this era of instant worldwide communication, no warning was given to the people."

The announcer and his backdrop disappeared and were replaced by images of the aftermath of a terrible flood: a gigantic boat sitting on its side in the middle of a street, a train overturned, cars all piled up like toys that had been tossed by an angry child, buildings knocked down, people rummaging through rubble and garbage, demolished buildings . . . and bodies . . . lots of bodies . . . lying face down in the street. A mother was screaming and crying uncontrollably, a dead child in her arms. Bodies hung limply from the limb of a tree; arms and legs stuck out of the mud or peeked out from beneath mountains of debris.

"Beth! Beth?"

I started at the mention of my name. It was Tad . . . the phone. I bent down and picked it up from the floor.

"I'm here. It's awful."

"What channel are you watching?" he asked.

"Twenty-seven."

"Don't put down the phone. I'm going to switch to that station. Let me keep talking to you," he said.

I heard the sound of the TV on his end become the same sound I was listening to.

The anchor came back on the screen. "The number of deaths, at this time, can only be roughly estimated. Projections suggest that the number will rise to over eighty thousand."

I gasped.

"As more bodies are recovered this count continues to soar, and some experts are predicting that the total will surpass one hundred thousand within twenty-four hours. While the vast majority of those who were killed are citizens of the countries hit by the tsunami, there are reports that the death totals include people from more than thirty-seven countries worldwide, including most countries in western Europe, Canada, Australia, New Zealand, and, of course, the United States."

"Beth, are you still there?" Tad asked.

"I'm here," I mumbled.

"In Indonesia," the announcer said, "it is estimated that in excess of four hundred thousand people have been left homeless."

The picture changed to a scene shot from an airplane or helicopter. It showed what looked like the remains of a city. All of the buildings were flattened to the ground as far as the eye could see, from the water's edge up onto the land for hundreds and hundreds of yards. Then, in the middle, one building remained standing, though destroyed. White concrete posts supported a roof with minarets rising above it—it was a mosque.

"The tsunami hit the coast with a force estimated to be hundreds of times more powerful than the atom bomb that was dropped on Hiroshima," the announcer said solemnly. "This scene of total devastation was once a thriving town, home to over ten thousand people. Their homes are gone. Their fishing boats are gone. And, as yet, there is no way to know how many lives are also gone."

The camera continued to scan the landscape. A few people could be seen from the air. Some looked up toward the camera, one even waved, but most seemed to be almost in a trance, wandering amid the wreckage.

"This video was shot by a tourist standing on his fourth-floor balcony in Phuket, Thailand."

There was a scene of a giant wave racing up the beach. You could see a man talking to somebody, or maybe narrating what he was seeing. I couldn't tell what language he was speaking, but his voice got louder and more excited as the wave hit the beach and barreled over some palm trees and—

"Oh my God!" I gasped. I recognized the scene.

The water crashed up over the patio and enveloped the pool, carrying everything with it. There were shrieks and the sound of shattering glass and objects shattering together, and the man's voice got louder and louder and louder.

I reached over and turned the TV off. I could still hear it coming over the phone.

"Turn off your television," I said to Tad.

"What?"

"Turn off your TV!" I barked.

The sound died almost immediately.

"Beth, I'm sure your parents are okay."

"That was our resort," I said, my voice barely a whisper. "That's where we stay."

There was silence on the other end.

"Our bungalow is just over from the pool . . . it's on the beach . . . right on the beach."

"Beth, I'm coming down," Tad said. "I'll be there in less than two hours."

"No," I said. "Don't come here."

"I don't think you should be alone right now. I'll borrow my father's car and I'll be right—"

"No, don't come here. I'm going home. Meet me at my house." I went to hang up and then changed my mind. "Thank you for coming . . . thank you."

CHAPTER TEN

—

I pushed "redial" on the phone again. There was silence for a few seconds and then I could hear it trying to connect, trying to circle the world and reach a phone in Thailand. Twenty-five, thirty, maybe forty times I'd hit "redial" as I drove home from the dorm. Each time it was the same. I couldn't even get through to the international line—a busy signal was telling me that all the lines were taken. I knew if I just kept trying, sooner or later I'd get through. Maybe this time . . . a busy signal. I pushed "end" and put the phone down on the seat beside me.

I put both hands on the wheel. The roads were slick. It wouldn't help anybody if I ended up in the ditch. I just had to concentrate on the road, slow down, and pretend that everything was all right, even if I didn't know anything for sure.

I reached for the phone again—and stopped myself. Maybe there was no point in even trying right now. Perhaps it was the phone that wasn't working. I'd be home in a few minutes and I could try again from there. Maybe there would even be a message waiting for me from my parents, telling me that everything was okay, that they were fine.

Who was I kidding? If I couldn't get through to them, how did I expect them to get through to me? At my end, the problem was just that all the international lines were being tied up with hundreds of thousands of people doing what I was doing, desperately trying to make contact with somebody. At their end, there would be telephone lines down, maybe the whole infrastructure destroyed. How could I even hope that they'd been able to call me? And even if, by some fluke, they had got through, they would have tried to call my cellphone or my dorm room and not left a message at home.

I turned onto the street and saw our house, with Mom's car in the driveway. For a fleeting, illogical micro-second I thought, *Oh, she's home.* I pulled my car in behind hers and hurried to the door.

The house was quiet and empty. I had known that it would be—that it should be—but it just seemed wrong. I turned on the television, partly because I needed an update but more because I needed some background noise, to hear sounds, voices, so I wouldn't feel so alone.

When I picked up the phone it was beeping rapidly, indicating that there were messages. I felt a little surge of adrenaline. Maybe . . . just maybe. I punched in the code.

"*You have four new messages*," the electronic voice announced. "*Your first new message was sent at 7:30 a.m.*"

Who would call that early . . . except my parents!

I was disappointed to hear the voice of a partner at my father's law firm. "I know you're not there," he said. "I just didn't know what else to do. If you get this message, please call me as soon as possible . . . I know you're okay . . . just call me . . . okay?"

The second message was from a friend of my mother's saying almost the same thing. I fast-forwarded through it. The third message was from my aunt Amy asking them to call and saying how worried she was. I'd call her right away, as soon as I knew anything. One more call, one more chance. I'd begun to say a silent prayer when the strange voice started, telling us we could get "a Christmas carpet-cleaning special discount." I slammed the phone down.

"Hello!"

I jumped. It was Tad.

"I'm in here!"

Tad rushed into the room and threw his arms around me. It felt good. Very good.

"Are you all right?" he asked.

"I'm here. I'm not the one we need to be worried about."

"I'm concerned about your family, but I'm still worried about you. What can I do to help?" he asked.

I shook my head. "I don't know what either of us can do."

"Whatever it is, we'll figure it out together. Have you been listening to any updates on the situation?"

Again I shook my head. "I just got here . . . I wasn't expecting you for a while . . . you're here so soon."

"I drove a little faster than I should have," he said. "Is there somebody you should call?"

"There's my aunt Amy, and one of the partners at my dad's firm, I guess. They both phoned."

"I mean to get information," he said. "Is there somebody you can call who can tell you what's happening in Thailand?"

"I don't know. Who do you think I should call?"

"The State Department, the U.S. embassy in Bangkok, maybe a reporter . . . come to think of it, my uncle works for *ABC News*. How about if I give him a call?"

"Could you do that?"

"Of course. I'll call him, and then I'll try to call the State Department. I know they're involved. The news said there were many American lives lost in every—" He stopped himself mid-sentence. "I'm sorry, that was insensitive. There have to be hundreds, maybe even *thousands* of Americans in those countries."

"Thousands," I agreed.

"And I can't even imagine anything happening to your father," Tad said. "Or him letting anything happen to your mother or brother."

I knew exactly what he meant. It wasn't just that my dad was big—he *was* a large man, though, and Sam was showing signs of catching up to him in height. It was that he always seemed to have things under control. Nothing bothered him. Nothing fazed him. He always knew what to do.

"I'm sure they're just fine. Probably the worst thing is that they can't get through to you to let you know that they're okay. Your mother was feeling really guilty before this happened so she's probably driving herself *nuts* right now."

Despite it all I laughed. I could imagine my mother pestering the hotel staff, demanding that they get a call through even if they had to dive down under water to get the phone. The MS had affected her body, but nothing could diminish her spirit.

"I'll go and make those calls," Tad said.

I showed him into my father's office and left him there. The sound of the TV in the other room drew me toward it. I sat down on the floor to watch.

A lot of the footage looked as though it had been shot with home video cameras. It was mostly short scenes, some of which seemed familiar to me already. There was an overturned train. Shots of a huge boat that had been picked up and carried far inland, and was now left high and dry with the retreat of the water. Scenes of waves overwhelming break walls and crushing trees, people desperately running for their lives, the whole thing punctuated by the sounds of screaming and yelling. There were rivers of water, so thick with debris that the surface was barely visible, racing between houses and buildings. Cars and buses were overturned, almost submerged, and people were clinging to them, clawing to get up, out of the water, trying to save their lives.

The scenes continued to roll and an unseen announcer began to speak.

"The death toll continues to rise. Preliminary estimates are that over one hundred thousand lives have been lost, making this one of the most deadly natural catastrophes in recorded human history. While these numbers are almost beyond belief, experts believe that the final tally could be twice as high as that. The wave destroyed roads, airports, rail lines, television and radio stations and relay towers, telephone lines and cellphone towers, and other methods of communication."

That's what I was thinking. They were fine but they couldn't call me because the telephones were gone.

"Central authorities in Sri Lanka, Thailand, and Indonesia report that they have not been able to make contact with more remote communities to ascertain the extent of damages and fatalities there. Thus far, these pictures, taken either by people on the ground at the time or by plane, provide the only visual record."

The picture behind him changed to the shots of devastation I'd already seen. Flattened buildings. It looked as if an entire town had been squashed by some kind of gigantic steamroller.

"And while the vast majority of the victims are nationals of the affected countries, there have been reports of deaths of people from close to forty countries worldwide. This is particularly a factor in the tourist resorts in

W
A
V
E

the south of Sri Lanka and in the resorts in Thailand. We now have a report, direct by satellite phone, from one such resort in Thailand.

Resort . . . Thailand. I suddenly sat up straighter.

"Hello, this is Peter Phillips here in the New York office," the announcer said. "Can you hear me?"

There was a delay of a few seconds before an answer came. "Yes, Peter, this is Caleb Sawyer, reporting from Phuket, Thailand."

Phuket. He was there, right where my parents and brother were.

"How would you describe things, Caleb?"

A few more seconds of delay. "It is a horrendous scene," he said. "Stores, homes, and hotels have been badly damaged or even completely destroyed. It is a scene of total and utter devastation."

In the background they were re-running the footage of the waves crashing up over the break wall of our resort. I crawled forward, trying to see things more closely, somehow thinking that maybe I could see my family, but hoping I wouldn't, as the wave overwhelmed people running up the beach and then washed over the patio and pool and blasted into the lobby.

"Unofficial death counts for Thailand suggest upwards of four thousand fatalities, with another two thousand still missing, over ten thousand injured and requiring medical attention, and upwards of fifty thousand people left homeless."

Thailand was a big country with millions of

people. Those deaths had to be all along the coast.

"Phuket has been one of the most severely hit," he said, and my heart sank.

"Thank you, Caleb, for your report," the announcer said. "And we will expect updates from you as more news becomes known."

"Thank you, Peter," the unseen voice replied.

I didn't want any more news. I had to fight the urge to turn the TV off. I just wanted to go up to my room, yank down the blinds, turn off the lights, and pull the covers over my head. Just stay under the covers and wait for my parents to come home. I couldn't do that. I had to hear everything.

"In the wake of the disaster is an even greater threat as diseases, some as simple as diarrhea, threaten to kill the weakened survivors who have little or no medical care and lack many of the basic necessities, including food and clean water. A massive international effort is already underway to provide aid for the afflicted areas."

The background showed gigantic bags of grain on a skid being loaded by forklift onto an airplane. Medical supplies were being gathered up by what looked like a couple of doctors or nurses.

"Doctors, nurses, and emergency personnel are being transported to the afflicted areas. Portable hospitals and water-purification systems are being flown in. There is a desperate need for help. Listed below are the numbers where donations can be made," the announcer said. "Please, reach down deep and offer your help."

That was it. I knew what I had to do. I ran upstairs to my parents' room and into their closet. There on the shelf were my father's old golf shoes. I reached inside and pulled out his bank book, an extra credit card, and a thick wad of cash. I didn't even need to count to know that it was two thousand dollars. It was for an emergency. If this wasn't an emergency, I didn't know what was. I stuffed all of it into my pocket. I had to make a phone call.

The phone book was in the front hall cupboard. I pulled it down and went back to the living room. I opened up the book, flipping pages until I found what I was looking for. I dialed the number. It was probably going to be busy. There had to be hundreds of people calling in. Hundreds. It started to ring! But that didn't mean they were going to pick it up.

"Come on, come on, be there . . . answer the phone," I pleaded.

"Hello, Thai Airways," the voice said.

"Yes, I need to book a flight to Thailand as soon as possible."

CHAPTER ELEVEN

—

"Beth, are you sure you want to do this?" Tad asked. He was driving, and his eyes were fixed on the road, but I could see by the expression on his face that he was worried.

"I don't have much choice."

"You could just stay home. That's another choice."

"I can't just sit at home and do nothing!"

"You could sit at home and do *something*."

"What could I do?"

"Make phone calls, or wait for someone to call you. What am I going to tell your parents when they call and you're already halfway to Thailand?" Tad asked.

"You'll tell them to call me so I know they're safe and that they should meet me at the airport."

"What time do you arrive?"

W
A
V
E

"It's a twenty-five-hour flight including a layover in Tokyo, and there's an eleven-hour time change . . . so . . . around five or six in the morning. And remember to tell them that I'm coming into Bangkok, not Phuket International."

Phuket International was the airport where we usually landed but it had been closed to incoming flights.

"By the way, thanks for volunteering to stay at my house and man the phones."

"It was the least I could do."

"And thanks for driving me to the airport, too."

"Again, no problem. How much time do we have . . . when does your flight leave?"

"It leaves at twenty after five so I need to be there . . ." I looked at my watch. "Soon."

"We *will* be there soon. Less than ten minutes. Do you want me to park and come inside with you?"

I shook my head. "There's no point. I have to get right through Security. Besides, I want you to get back to my place as quickly as you can, in case they call."

"Are you sure you have everything?"

"I think so. Passport, money, credit cards."

"Ticket?"

"Waiting at the counter."

"And do you really have everything you need in your purse and that little backpack?"

"I hope so." I wasn't checking any luggage. I had the two carry-on pieces—one big, the other small—and that was all I was taking. I needed to travel light.

Tad turned and we entered the grounds of the airport. Up above were signs directing us to Departures. This was all so familiar. It was only a few days ago that I'd been here dropping off my parents. That seemed hard to believe, as if it were a million years ago.

We pulled up in front of the doors. As I went to climb out, Tad gently took my arm. "Are you sure you want to do this? Are you *really* sure?"

"I'm positive."

But I wasn't nearly as sure as I was trying to sound. I knew this might turn out to be the completely wrong thing to do—a waste of time and money, almost three thousand dollars for the ticket. They were probably just fine, and if they weren't, what could I do? Okay, it probably *wasn't* the smartest thing in the world to do, but I had to do it.

"How are you going to find them?" he asked.

"I don't know. I'll figure that out when I get there. I just know I'll find them. I will."

He wrapped his arms around me. It felt safe and warm and good. I could just stay here and wait. I could . . .

No, I couldn't.

The plane touched down in Bangkok. It had been twenty-seven hours since we'd left New York. The plane had been delayed a little during the layover in Tokyo, and then we'd circled over Bangkok for more than an hour before we were finally able to set down. The flight attendant had explained that there was increased air traffic because of all the relief planes landing with aid. It was reassuring to know that there was help coming, but frustrating to wait in line to land. I needed to get on the ground.

As we taxied along the runway I turned on my cell-phone. It had been ages since I'd been able to check for messages, and now I was hoping for magic. I'd turn on the phone and it would ring and it would be my father, or Tad, telling me he'd spoken to my parents. I'd just have to wait a few minutes for that call to come through.

Next I took off my watch. It wasn't eight-thirty in the evening on December 27. It was seven-thirty in the morning, and the date was December 28. I changed the time.

The plane came to a stop and the little seat belt light went out. I pulled my backpack out from under the seat in front of me and got to my feet, along with everybody else. There were lots of empty seats—many more than there were passengers. I'd been worried about not getting on a flight out, but I needn't have been concerned. The airlines had put on extra planes to bring people home, and, as the attendant selling me the ticket had explained, tourists were all trying to *leave* Thailand, not *arrive.* So this plane would arrive half empty and leave completely filled up, with more people waiting to get on the next flight.

That might make it hard for us to get a plane back to New York immediately, but I didn't care. Once we were all together, it wouldn't matter. If I knew my father, he probably wouldn't even want to leave. He'd probably suggest we find someplace, well away from the beach, that was still operating and just finish out the holiday. Maybe I would spend at least part of the Christmas holidays with my family. I knew my swim coach might be angry, but he was the least of my worries.

People were on their feet, getting their bags from the overhead compartments. It wasn't the usual crowd of people, shoulder to shoulder, and I was able to ease my way past them so I could be almost the first person off. The door opened and bright light and warm air flooded in as people exited.

I stopped for a split second at the door. There was a set of stairs pushed up to the plane and we were exiting onto the tarmac. I could see that we had come to a stop well away from the terminal. I climbed down and a flight attendant was at the bottom, directing us toward the building. It was surrounded by planes, and other aircraft dotted the tarmac. Most were commercial planes, but I could also see big military aircraft, and there were men and machines unloading skids laden with what I hoped were relief supplies. Farther away was a whole fleet of helicopters. That made sense. I knew that the airport in Phuket was closed. The helicopters would probably be used to ferry the supplies from here to there . . . and getting from here to there was *my* next challenge, as well.

Here I was in Bangkok. All I needed was a way to get to Phuket. I figured the answer was somewhere inside the terminal. I followed the little line of people inside. Most went off in one direction to claim their luggage. Everything I needed was in my carry-on bags.

I skidded to a stop. Inside the terminal there were people everywhere. It wasn't that I didn't know about crowds. I lived in New York, after all. I'd traveled through airports around the world. But this was different.

All of the seats in the waiting areas were taken, and people were sitting and lying on the floor. The place was jammed to the rafters with tourists—most of them very noticeably white in an Asian country, and all of them wanting to get home. Some were in filthy clothes, or their hair was all matted and sticking up in a thousand directions. Others were in mismatched clothing or looked as if they'd just come off the beach and had nothing to change into.

Despite the size of the crowd there was hardly any noise. The normal buzz of an airport was somehow missing. Instead there was an eerie silence. People were speaking in quiet tones, as though they were in a church or at a funeral. A funeral. How many of these people had lost somebody? I didn't have time to think about any of that. I couldn't think about anything except what I had to do. I had to keep moving.

I passed by a long line of people waiting to use a bank of pay phones. People were trying to call home. I thought about my parents maybe waiting in a similar line somewhere trying to do the same thing . . . somewhere . . . they could be here! Quickly I scanned the line, looking for my father or mother or even my brother—my father might be sitting somewhere with my mother and they would have let my brother call. I looked around. I didn't see them.

But what did I expect? Did I really think that I'd just flown halfway around the world to bump into them standing at a pay phone the second I got off a plane? The odds against that happening were astronomical. But what were the odds of them being *somewhere* in this airport? Those odds had to be better. There had to be thousands and thousands of people here. And, since the airport in Phuket was closed, wouldn't this be where my parents would go to catch a flight home? Maybe the odds had shifted in my favor.

I didn't know how big the airport was but I had to somehow make my way around the whole thing. My family might be sitting in three of the hard plastic seats, waiting for a flight or a chance to call home. I stopped just walking and started to look. Each face, each person was one more chance. Aisle by aisle I walked, letting my eyes linger on every person, in the seats, huddled together, or stretched out on the floor. These people were just like us—tourists— and they might have come from the same resort in Phuket.

Up ahead my attention was grabbed by a large white banner, more like a sheet, with the word "HELP" crudely written in big black letters. Help was what I needed. Maybe somebody there could help me. I kept looking at the people as I passed by but worked my way toward that counter.

As I got closer I noticed that the counter was flanked by a gigantic bulletin board. On it were dozens—no, hundreds—of handwritten messages. I read the first: "*Tammy and Brent are fine. Looking for our friend Suzie— call home and leave a message. Leaving on 7:30 flight to Tokyo.*"

Almost all of the notices listed names of people who were being looked for, or just told people that somebody was fine, alive. There were messages in different languages—besides English, there was French, German, Italian, Swedish, and some languages that had strange letters or scripts that I didn't recognize.

"Can I help you?"

It was my turn.

"My parents . . . my brother . . . I'm looking for them."

"What are their names?" the man asked.

"My parents are James and Ingrid Brooks, and my brother is Sam."

"How old is your brother?"

"He's twelve . . . almost thirteen."

He made a few notes and then started flipping through a thick stack of papers. He stopped at one page and ran his finger down the list.

He looked up. "I don't see them," he said. "That doesn't mean a lot, though."

"What *does* it mean?"

"This is a list of people who have come through this airport in the last two days. It was updated about an hour ago. What part of Thailand were they in?"

"Phuket."

He shook his head. "There aren't many people here from Phuket yet. They're still being cared for on the island. How did you get here?"

"I flew."

"From Phuket?" he asked.

"My *family* is in Phuket. I just flew in from New York."

He looked shocked.

"I came to try to find them. I have to get to Phuket."

"That's not going to be possible. There are no flights."

"There have to be *some* flights."

"Nothing is going to Phuket except for food and medical supplies," he said.

"But there have to be some flights. They are bringing people here, right?"

"People come *back* when the emergency supplies are unloaded. They're bringing people away from the disaster area, not to it . . . unless they're medical personnel, or people needed to help with the cleanup."

"I could help."

"The best way you can help is to stay put here and wait for your family to come to you."

"I just can't wait. There has to be *some* way."

He shrugged. "I can save you time by telling you not to bother trying to book a flight. They're not flying anybody surplus into the area. And the only way to get there now is by road."

"How far is it?"

"Just over five hundred miles."

"That's not too far," I said, talking more to myself than to him.

"That's a twelve-hour drive, under normal circumstances, and these aren't normal circumstances. It would

W
A
V
E

119

take at least twice that long right now, and that's assuming that you could even find a car to rent or somebody to drive you. I'm sorry, but there really isn't any choice. You should just stay here and wait."

I felt a rush of anger. I wanted to yell at him or argue or fight with him, but what was the point? It wasn't his fault, and there was nothing I could do to convince him or prove that he was wrong. He *was* probably right.

"I'm sorry I can't do more," he said.

"I understand."

"I want you to keep checking back here every hour as we update the arrival list," he said. "Look at the message board. You never can tell what information might show up there. And I was told that later on today we're going to be given copies of lists from other parts of the country, including Phuket."

"So, my parents could be on one of those lists?" I asked hopefully.

"We'll hope they're on the good list."

"The good list?"

"The one listing the survivors."

I felt as though I'd been slapped in the face. The list with survivors. Not the list of the dead. How could he even think that my parents might be on that list?

"Check back later," he said.

"Thank you," I mumbled, and started to wander away. I was in a daze, as if there was a fog surrounding me. I needed to sit down, but there was no place to sit. Even every square foot of floor was taken, and—

"You want to go to Phuket?"

I turned around to see a man in his thirties. His pale skin was marked by freckles and smudges of dirt, and he had dreadlocks sticking out from under his dirty baseball cap. He was wearing equally dirty shorts and T-shirt, and he looked as though he hadn't shaved in days. His eyes were red, tired, and a little crazed-looking. All in all, he looked like the sort of person I'd cross the street to avoid in New York.

"Well, do you want to go to Phuket?" he asked again. I couldn't make out the accent . . . Australian, or maybe South African. He could have been from New Zealand.

"Yes," I answered hesitantly.

He leaned in close. He smelled of sweat. "Best come with me," he hissed in my ear. His breath was as foul as his body odor.

He turned and started to walk away. I stood there watching, not moving, unsure of what to do. He turned back and scowled and shook his head sadly.

"You coming or what?" he called out.

I didn't move.

"Your loss." He turned and started walking again.

I knew what the smart thing to do was. I ran after him instead.

W
A
V
E

CHAPTER TWELVE

—

I followed behind him, close but at a safe distance, as he walked through the crowded terminal. What could happen here with all these people around? He stopped at a door that read "AUTHORIZED PERSONNEL ONLY." He looked back at me, glanced around him, and then opened it. He held the door open and gestured for me to enter. I stopped at the threshold.

"Should I be going in there? It says 'Authorized Personnel'—"

"I'm authorizing you."

Hesitantly I stepped in. We were behind the scenes in what looked like a baggage area. There was nobody to be seen, and I suddenly felt very uneasy. But as he kept walking, I kept following. What else could I do? I dropped a few more feet back, just in case I had to run. My mind started to race, thinking about who this man was and how stupid it was to follow him into a deserted place.

He stopped and turned around. "You'd better put this on," he said, and he handed me the jacket he'd been carrying.

"I'm . . . I'm not cold," I mumbled.

"But you *do* want to get to Phuket, don't you?"

"Yeah, but—"

"Then put on the jacket."

I took it from him. It was a cheap vinyl rain jacket. There was something written on the back. I stretched it out. In big, white, fluorescent letters it said "RESCUE."

"I couldn't help overhearing your conversation at the help counter. You need to get to Phuket, and I'm going to Phuket."

"You're going to drive me?"

He laughed. "Do I look like a flipping taxi driver?" he asked.

"No."

"I'm a pilot. I'm going to fly you."

Actually, he looked more like a taxi driver than he did a pilot.

"But if we're flying, why aren't we going out to the tarmac?" I asked nervously.

"We are. It's just that they wouldn't let you out there through the main doors. They're checking everybody's ID. We're gonna have to sort of smuggle you out through the side door. Put on the jacket and come with me." He started to walk away.

W
A
V
E

I slipped it on and ran and caught up to him.

"By the way, if anybody asks you, tell them you're a doctor."

"A doctor?"

"Um . . . maybe you are too young a sheila to be a doctor. Say you're a nurse. Tell 'em you were hired by the Thai government and you came all the way from . . . where *did* you come from?"

"New York."

"All the way from the States to help. Makes you sound like a genuine heroine instead of a criminal or a smuggler or a looter." He pulled off his baseball cap and put it on my head. "Just keep your head down, try not to say anything you don't need to say, and stay close, okay?"

I adjusted the cap and nodded in agreement.

He pushed open a little door and light streamed in. We stepped out and onto the tarmac, almost directly beneath the belly of a big commercial jet. There were men running around and machines loading luggage into the plane. Nobody seemed to pay any attention to us as they continued to work.

We moved along the lip of the tarmac, right beside the terminal, past plane after plane, until we came to the area I'd seen when we landed. There were hundreds of skids of supplies, some much higher than my head. Forklift trucks and men carrying individual bags were moving the supplies. We moved through the middle of the action and I felt very conspicuous.

"Act like you own the place," he said to me. "Wave to the people."

"What?"

"Wave, it's not hard." He waved at a couple of the men and they waved back. "Like that. It's easy."

I looked over and waved, and they smiled and waved back, which brought a smile to my face too.

There was a line of helicopters at the edge of the tarmac. They were of all types and sizes, painted different colors and belonging to various organizations. Alongside Thai army helicopters were some that bore the United Nations logo, while others had the Stars and Stripes of the United States proudly painted on the side. I felt a lot safer seeing them, and the soldiers that went with them.

"There's me girl," he said.

In among the big military helicopters sat a little one, painted bright red, and on its side it said "THAILAND AIR TOURS."

"You fly a tour helicopter?" I asked.

"That's what I'd be doing now, if it weren't for all of this," he said. "Government hired every chopper they could find, including mine."

There were men loading bags into the side door of his helicopter.

"How's it going, mates?" he asked.

"Perfect timing," one of them said. He had the same accent. "Just putting on the last bags." He looked at me. "Who's this?"

"What if I told you she was a nurse?" he asked.

"I'd think she's too young to be a nurse."

"How about if I said she was my sheila?"

"I'd think she was too good looking to hook up with an old piece of driftwood like you, so that one's even less believable."

"Then the nurse story it is," he said. "Agreed?"

"Agreed," the man answered.

He circled around the little cockpit of the helicopter and climbed in.

"You come on here," the other man said as he opened the Plexiglas door to the co-pilot's seat. "Best ride up front, the back is stuffed to the roof."

I threw my bags in and climbed up gingerly. He closed the door behind me and turned the handle to lock it—I *hoped* to lock it. The pilot was going through the controls, hitting switches and pushing buttons. I realized I didn't even know his name.

"I'm Beth," I said.

"I'm Steve. Pleased to meet you." He reached over-top of me and I squirmed in my seat.

"Seat belt," he said kindly. "You need your seat belt."

"Oh . . . yeah . . . of course." I felt embarrassed.

It ran around my waist and over both shoulders. He snapped it into place and then went back to fiddling with the controls. Little lights on the dashboard came to life and the rotors overhead slowly started to spin. He put on his headset and spoke to the control tower. I could hear only his side of the conversation, and he was using some sort of shorthand aviation code. That, combined with his thick accent and the growing roar of the rotors as they spun faster and faster meant that I really couldn't hear much at all, and what I could hear I didn't understand.

Steve the pilot gave a thumbs-up to the man standing beside the chopper and he returned the sign. The noise got louder again and we lifted off the ground. It was slow. It felt like riding in an elevator—a glass-sided elevator. We kept going up until we were high enough off the ground for me to see around and past the other helicopters. The whole tarmac was a beehive of activity. People and planes, helicopters, forklifts, and what seemed like thousands of skids of supplies.

"Ever been in a helicopter before?" Steve yelled above the roar of the engine.

"No, never," I yelled back.

"Greatest ride on earth. You had anything to eat lately?"

"Not for three or four hours."

"Good. No food on the stomach means less chance of you upchucking and me having to clean out my chopper. Do you know how hard it is to get rid of the smell? Stays with you for flight after flight."

"I don't get airsick."

"Even better. Hang on to your hat . . . or, I guess, my hat."

Before I could reply or react, we dipped to the side and sped off. I grabbed onto the seat with both hands. We skipped just over the top of the trees on the outskirts of the airport.

"We're pretty low," I said.

"What?"

"We're low!" I said loudly, trying to be heard above the rotors.

"Gotta fly low until we get away from the airport. Don't wanna get into the flight paths of any of the big birds. Could be hazardous to our health."

We passed over some houses. We were so low that I could see people walking on the streets. They looked up and waved, but we were moving so fast that before I could wave back they were gone.

"How long will it take to get there?" I asked.

"Just under two hours!" he yelled back. "This is my fifteenth trip in the last two days."

"Fifteen! When did you get time to sleep?"

"Haven't had much of that. Could you do me a favor?" he asked.

"Sure."

"If I fall asleep during the flight could you either wake me up or take over the controls?"

He had a dead-serious look on his face that dissolved into a smile, and he started laughing, really hard. Maybe it was a joke, but it wasn't that funny, and it wasn't making me feel any better about how tired he actually was. I'd just keep talking to him and make sure he didn't fall asleep.

"I still don't understand why they won't let me go to Phuket," I said.

"Government policy. Nobody in. They're afraid of looters, criminals coming in and taking advantage of the situation. I've even heard tales of people kidnapping young children who have had their parents killed."

"That's awful! I can't imagine people doing that."

"I was hearing about a case in Sri Lanka. They found a baby, and now four different couples have come forward claiming he's their son."

"That's incredible."

"Saddest thing is that all four really believe it. Think about that, four couples who lost a child, a boy about the same age, all thinking it's their baby."

"But they can't all really believe that, can they?"

"Human beings believe what they need to believe. They don't want to accept that their child is lost so they have to believe this is their son."

"How will they figure out who's telling the truth . . . or, I guess, who's right . . . anyway, whose son it is?"

"Simple. DNA test. Same way they're identifying the bodies that they're finding that don't have any identification. There have been hundreds found like that, and . . ." He stopped and looked over at me. "You don't need to be hearing this stuff right now. Bottom line is people are capable of some pretty awful things. A disaster like this brings out the worst *and* the best in people."

"I don't understand . . . the best?"

"I've been hearing tales of people risking their lives for complete strangers."

I could picture my father doing that.

"Most of the tourists have left, but some have insisted on staying, and they're helping to search for survivors, tending to the injured."

"My mother is a nurse. She'd do that."

This was good—now I had another positive image to hold on to. I could almost see my mother and father helping survivors and trying to make a terrible situation better. Maybe Sam would even be helping with the cleanup. I hoped there'd be something like that I could do, some way to make myself useful.

"Can I ask you another question?" I said.

"Shoot."

"Why are you bringing me to Phuket?"

He shrugged. "Figured you weren't a criminal or a looter. Just thought you were somebody worried about her family. You just wanted to do what I'd want to do if it were my family. That's all."

"Thanks."

"No need."

"Could you get in trouble for doing this?" I asked.

"Maybe I could. Wouldn't be the first time. Besides, what are they going to do to me? It's not like they can fire me, because I don't work for anybody but myself."

We were flying just above the treetops but not that much higher. Below us was lush, green jungle, dotted with houses and lined by roads.

"It all just looks normal," I said.

"Here it is. It's only when we get to the coast that you'll notice anything. When was the last time you slept?" he asked.

"I caught a few hours on the plane."

"You must be beat. Maybe you should close your eyes and catch a few winks," he suggested.

Yeah, like that was going to happen. My thoughts were racing, my heart was aching, and I was looking out at the most spectacular view I had ever seen in my life. Even though I was exhausted, sleep was the last thing on my mind. Which was okay, because I wasn't the one flying this helicopter.

"Maybe you should sleep, too . . . I mean, once we land," I said.

"Believe me, if I go to sleep up here we'll land soon enough!" He started laughing again. "Beautiful country, isn't it?" he said.

"It is. Probably the most beautiful place in the world."

"That's what makes it even more tragic. You know how beautiful it was. And now . . ." He let the sentence trail off. "We're coming up to the coast right now."

In the distance I could see the green of the jungle give way to the blue of the ocean. Between the two was a thin line of brown, the beach. It all looked so natural, so normal. At least from up here.

As Steve closed the distance to the ocean I started to realize that things *weren't* so normal. The beach wasn't a thin line. It got thicker and thicker, wider and wider, and it wasn't open beach, it was littered with logs and debris. The trees at the edge of the beach had all been flattened or snapped or had simply disappeared. I tried to imagine the power of a wave that could do that. I couldn't.

"See the fishing boats?" he asked.

I looked toward the ocean. There were half a dozen boats out on the water.

"Those are the lucky ones," Steve said. "When the tsunami hit, they were out fishing."

"How does that make them lucky?"

"Boats that were in harbor, tied up to docks, or even on the shore, were smashed. Those out on the ocean survived."

"But that doesn't make sense. Shouldn't they have been hit by the wave first? Shouldn't they have gotten hit the worst, with nothing to protect them?"

"That's not how a tsunami works. Out in the deep ocean the wave is deep, too. A ship out there would feel only a slight bump, maybe a foot or three, as the wave passed underneath. I've talked to people who were out on cruise ships, even snorkeling when the wave hit. They didn't feel anything," Steve said. "It's when it hits shallow water that the wave starts to slow down *and* pile up. Do you know what the word 'tsunami' means?"

I shook my head. "It's Japanese, right?"

"It's Japanese for 'harbor wave.' Way back in Japanese history, there were stories of fishing boats going out and coming back to find whole villages gone because of the wave that hit the harbor. Speaking of which, look to the left."

I looked down and over. I didn't really see anything.

"See that little inlet?"

"Yeah?"

"Three days ago there was a nice little fishing village down there."

"But I can't see anything."

"There's nothing left of the village to see. The whole thing was just picked up and washed away. It's like some giant just grabbed it, stuck it in his pocket, and walked off with it. The only hints are in the trees. Maybe you can pick something out."

I strained my eyes. "I can't see anything."

"Look farther in, well away from the water."

I looked, scanning back and forth, and . . . I could see colors but I couldn't make out exactly what they were. "Are those boats?"

"About half a dozen. Some are caught up in the trees. They were tied up when the wave hit and washed that far inland. Gives you an idea about the wave. You know, there were over two hundred people in that village. I don't know if any survived."

I couldn't comprehend how a village could simply vanish, how boats could be washed into trees, how two hundred people could cease to exist. If that was what happened here, could it have been any different at the resort? How could my family possibly have survived?

"Strange," Steve said, "a little harbor, an inlet—what makes it safer for boats during a storm makes it worse when there's a tsunami. It only amplifies the waves, makes 'em higher."

"So it wasn't that bad everywhere?"

"Not everywhere. The height of the waves depended on the depth of the water and the contours of the land."

I tried to think of the beach in front of the resort. I could picture it in my mind. It was long and straight, no inlet, no contours. And you could walk out a long way before it went over your head. It was shallow, which meant the waves would pile even higher.

"There's Phuket right up ahead," Steve said.

CHAPTER THIRTEEN

—

The helicopter dropped and banked toward my side, and I was practically pinned against its Plexiglas canopy. Thank goodness for the seat belt.

"That's where I'm landing," Steve said as he flattened it out again.

Straight ahead here was a large open area of green and in the middle, crudely drawn, a giant X. We were close enough that I could see that there was already another, bigger helicopter on the ground. I could also see trucks and skids and tiny figures all bustling around.

"Remember, when we land, if anybody asks, you're a nurse."

"But what if they ask me to help somebody?"

"That could be a problem. Fake it the best you

can and tell them the person needs to see a doctor."

"I can't do that. I'd just be making it all up!"

"No worries. Everybody should see a doctor. If you say that, you won't be hurting anybody. You might even save a life."

The forward motion of the chopper stopped and my stomach stayed up as we dropped. Steve set his chopper down gently on the ground.

"There, perfect landing," he said.

"I hardly felt it."

"Years of ferrying around tourists gives you a gentle touch."

Almost instantly the back door was flung open and a man jumped in and started to grab the bags of supplies.

"Sorry I can't get you any closer to the resort area than this," Steve said.

"This is just great. Maybe I can get a ride from here."

"Not likely. Can't get a ride from here without explaining who you are. Besides, lots of the roads leading to the resorts are blocked. Walking is the only way to get around. It's not far. Two, maybe three miles."

I undid the seat belt and wiggled the door handle, trying to get out.

"Push it down and then out," Steve said.

I followed his instructions and the door opened.

"What have you got in those bags?" he asked.

"Clothes, personal things . . . why?"

"No food or water?"

"No," I said. "I thought I could pick up something when I got here."

"Nothing to get. Dump out most of it. I'll go and see if I can rustle you up some stuff."

Steve climbed out of the cockpit leaving me alone— that is, except for the men who were unloading the helicopter. They were moving incredibly fast, passing the sacks from person to person and then piling them up on top of a wooden skid. I tried not to let them see me looking, tried to avoid eye contact. I didn't want anybody to ask me any questions.

I took everything out of my backpack except one change of clothes, an extra pair of shoes, and my toiletry items. I tried to fold the rest into a little pile at my feet and then thought better of it. What was the point?

Steve came back with his arms full of . . . something. "Here you go," he said. "These will keep you hydrated and fed." He had five large bottles of water and lots of little foil packages, which he dumped on the helicopter's seat.

"Don't drink the water, any water that isn't in a bottle," he said. "The whole filtration system is filled with seawater and sewage. And these are army rations." He held up one of the little packages. "Each energy bar is a meal. They taste like sawdust but they're filled with energy. Two of these are good for a day's worth of calories." There had to be twenty or thirty of them on the seat.

"I won't need that many."

"Better to take more than not have enough when you need them. Besides, you might be providing food for your whole family, and who knows who else. No telling what the food situation is like where they're holed up."

I started to put them in my backpack. There'd be enough space for everything now.

"I'd better give you back your jacket."

"No, best you hang onto it. No telling how that jacket might help you get someplace you need to go. Besides, it goes nice with your eyes. But I could use my lucky hat back."

"Oh, I'm sorry, I forgot I was even wearing it." I took the hat off and handed it to him, and he put it back on his head.

"I don't know how to thank you," I said. "For everything. I just don't know what to say."

"You don't have to say anything now. Save the thank-you for when I drop you and your family off in Bangkok."

"You'd be willing to fly us back?"

"I have plenty of space on the return trips. Besides, you didn't think I'd just bring you down here and abandon you, did you?"

I threw my arms around him and gave him a big hug.

"You just find your way back here and wait for me. If I'm not here I'll be dropping back in three, maybe four hours. Now you go and find your family."

I gave him one more hug and then climbed out. I took a few steps and looked back. Steve was already pitching in, helping to unload the chopper so he could head back out again.

"Steve!" I yelled, and he looked over. "Get some *sleep*, okay?"

He smiled, nodded, and gave me the thumbs-up.

I made my way through the men and machines that were buzzing all around. I kept my head down and walked through the field. A building off to one side looked like a school, and then I got it—this airport was a schoolyard. At both ends were crudely made soccer posts, and there was a baseball diamond in the far corner.

I got on to the road and started to walk. I was grateful to have got away without any awkward questions. I hurried around the corner, anxious to get out of sight.

The road was rough, and there was thick vegetation on both sides. I'd been to Thailand so many times over the years, but it struck me that this was the very first time I'd ever walked anywhere by myself. In fact, aside from being in the washroom, this might have been the first time I'd ever *been* by myself here. I was always with one of my parents, or my brother, or other guests or hotel staff or people in the stores. Here, it was just me and the trees and bush. There was nothing else . . . except for the cell-phone tower at the top of the hill!

I pulled out my phone and flipped it open. It was getting a signal. Why hadn't my parents tried to reach me? Why hadn't Tad called? Maybe they just couldn't get through. Then it dawned on me that *I* could try to call, too.

There was no point in trying to reach my parents at the resort. Even if the phones were working I doubted they'd still be there. But by now they must have been able to reach a phone and they should have been able to call Tad. I started to dial home.

There was silence. Was the phone trying to make a connection or was it dead? Was that the reason nobody had called me, because they couldn't? I wanted to talk to somebody, but if they couldn't reach me, that might mean that they were all right and they just couldn't tell me . . . It started to ring.

"Hello!"

"It's me."

"Beth! I was trying to call you!" Tad exclaimed.

"You heard from my parents?" I asked hopefully.

"No, no, nothing," he said, and my heart fell. "I just needed to know where you were, what was happening. I've been trying all evening but the international lines are all busy and I was worried sick, not knowing and wondering if you were okay and—"

"I'm okay," I said. "I'm in Phuket."

"It looks awful," he said. "I mean, on the news. The whole beach area is a disaster."

"I'm not on the beach. I just landed. I'm inland and walking toward the coast. It's less than three miles from here. I just hoped you'd heard from my parents."

"They probably just can't get to a phone," Tad said. "They said that the whole phone system along the coast has been wiped out."

Somehow that was reassuring. It wasn't that anything had happened to them, it was the phones. Like all those people lined up at the phones at the Bangkok Airport—they wouldn't be able to call until they got that far.

"You've been following it on the news," I said.

"It's on every channel. They're saying it's the biggest natural disaster in the history of the world. They keep upping the death counts. They think it could be over two hundred thousand people killed."

I think Tad and I both heard what he said at the same time.

"But not that many in Thailand!" he exclaimed. "That's mainly in other places . . . Sri Lanka and Indonesia were hit the hardest. And India and the Maldives and Malaysia. There have even been deaths in Kenya and Tanzania. Thailand wasn't the worst hit, not even close."

I knew what he was doing, trying to make me feel better. I also knew he wouldn't be lying. But still, I had to ask, I had to know.

"How bad was Thailand hit?" I asked.

There was a pause. "Pretty bad."

"How many deaths?"

There was an even longer pause. "I don't know exactly . . . I don't think they really know yet."

"How many do they know?"

"Five thousand dead," he said quietly. "Another three thousand still missing and over ten thousand injured."

I felt my whole body go limp as a shiver ran through it, in spite of the heat. I needed to sit down. I slumped to the ground.

"Those are almost all local people," Tad said.

I could tell by his voice that he was scrambling to make me feel better. It wasn't working, but I was glad he was trying. I had to hold on to something.

"The reports are of whole villages being wiped out," Tad said.

"I've seen one."

"You have?"

"From the air. I came in by helicopter. There was nothing left of it."

"That's why the total is so high," he said.

I started to do a calculation in my head. Steve had said that there were over two hundred people in that village . . . how many villages would have to be destroyed to make five thousand people? That would be twenty-five villages. All I had to do was hope that twenty-five villages were wiped out and—I stopped myself.

Here I was hoping, practically pleading, bargaining, calculating that innocent people had been killed—people I didn't even know—so that in my head it increased the odds of my family being alive. All those people were somebody's family, maybe they were whole families.

I had to ask Tad one more question. It was one I didn't want the answer to, but there was no choice.

"Are there reports of tourists being killed?"

"Yes." His answer was sudden and short.

"Americans?"

"Yes."

"How many?"

"Not that many. There were a lot from Sweden, over two hundred Swedish tourists are confirmed—"

"I don't care about Swedish tourists!" I snapped. "How many Americans?"

"They really don't know for sure yet—"

"Tad, how many?"

"Nine confirmed dead. Another fifty still missing. But that doesn't mean dead or anything because everything is so confused that they just can't find people yet."

He sounded almost panic-stricken. He didn't deserve my being angry and difficult with him. It wasn't his fault.

"Tad . . . thank you for being there," I said.

"I just wish I could be with you *there*. I shouldn't have let you go alone. I should have gone with you."

"You're helping me more where you are. Please, just call me as soon as you hear something."

"I'll try, but you call too! I might have news but not be able to get through to you, so you keep calling me. Promise?"

"I'll call."

"Not just if you hear anything, but just because. Promise me you'll try to call me later on today."

"I'll call," I said. "But you shouldn't worry if you don't hear from me. I'm heading down to the coast. Maybe there won't be any service down there."

"I understand," Tad said. "Be careful, and remember, I'm here, and if you need me I could be there, I could come over."

"I appreciate that. I appreciate everything. I've got to go. I'll talk to you later."

I was just about to put it away when I checked the power level. I still had three bars—enough for at least a couple of days. I wouldn't need any more than that. I hoped.

CHAPTER FOURTEEN

—

The road didn't stay deserted for long. There were people, in ones and twos or in bigger groups, moving up the road, coming toward me. They were all local people, Thais. Some were friendly and smiled and said a few words in English. They acted the way I was used to Thai people acting. Others were very different. Their heads were down, eyes on the ground, and it was as though they didn't even notice me as I passed. Some looked up, but they didn't seem to see. Their eyes were empty, their expressions blank. I didn't even want to think about what those eyes had seen and what had caused such a reaction.

I heard the sound of a vehicle and turned around, but I didn't see anything coming. The noise got louder and I realized it was coming from up ahead. A truck appeared, slowly bumping up the road. I moved to the side to allow it to pass.

The truck came to a stop right beside me and the driver leaned out the window.

"Do you need a ride?" he asked. He was Thai but his English was perfect.

"You're headed in the wrong direction for me. I'm looking for my family. They were down at a resort right on the beach."

"Not much left down there," the driver said. "I'm going up to the airfield. These people are going home."

"People?"

He gestured. "In the back. I'm bringing tourists from the evacuation site up to—"

"Can I check in the back? Please!"

"Of course. Sure."

He climbed out of the truck and I followed him around the side. The truck was canvas-covered, but the back was open. There were people sitting on benches along both sides.

"This girl is looking for her family," the driver called out.

A couple of faces peeked out of the back, but nobody I knew.

He turned to me. "What is the family name?"

"Brooks . . . James and Ingrid, and my brother is Sam."

"Are the Brookses on board?" the driver asked. "Does anybody know the Brookses or have any information about what happened to them?"

There was no answer, but I could hear a hum of conversation inside the truck.

"Where were they staying?" a voice called out.

"On the coast at a . . . at a resort," I stammered. "Kamala Bay Beach Resort."

"I was there," I heard a voice answer. A man came to the back and leaned out. "My wife and son and I, we were there. Do you have a picture of your family?"

"Yes! Yes, I do!" I pulled off my backpack and rummaged through it until I found my purse. I opened it up and pulled out our Christmas picture from the year before—it had been taken at the resort. That made me shudder. I passed it up.

The man looked at the picture and his eyes widened. He said something in a foreign language—maybe German— and a woman holding a baby appeared beside him. She looked at the picture and nodded.

"That is him, both of them," the man said. "The man and the boy."

"That's my father and brother. Have you seen them?"

"They are the ones who saved my wife and son. They are the ones."

The woman started to cry.

"They pulled them from the water," the man said. "They risked their lives . . . so brave."

"Do you know where they are? Do you know where they've gone?" I exclaimed. I felt such a rush of excitement and joy—if they'd saved these people then they had to be all right!

The man shook his head. "I saw them . . . I thanked them for what they had done, but then we left. My wife, my son . . . I had to get them to see a hospital, I mean, to see a doctor . . . we left. I am so sorry . . . I just wish I could tell more."

"You've done enough. At least I know they're alive, and that's all that matters."

He opened his mouth to say something and then he didn't.

"What? What were you going to say?" I asked.

"We left just as the second wave hit. There were four waves. We were away from the hotel, well up from the beach, but still, that second wave was much stronger than the first." He looked serious, deadly serious, but he stopped talking.

"And?"

"When I spoke to your father and your brother they were going down to the water, I think to help other people. When the next wave hit they might have been right on the beach. I don't know. I just do not wish to worry you."

I felt my knees buckle and my stomach churn violently. I had to fight the urge to simply collapse. But I couldn't . . . I needed to know more.

"And . . . and . . . my mother. Do you know anything about my mother?"

He said something to his wife that I didn't understand and then turned back to me.

"She was the one who held our son when they went

to save my wife. She was not with them at the beach. She must have stayed up at the hotel . . . lots of people were there in the lobby."

There was at least a glimmer of hope. "Thank you so much."

"No, no, thank you and your family. I wish I could do something to help, but I do not . . . wait!" He reached into his pocket and pulled out a wad of money. "You must take this!"

"I have money."

"Please, please, take it. We are leaving. This might help."

He stuffed the bills into my hand. I didn't want them, but he was so insistent, and maybe he was right, I might need them.

"And take this. It is my business card. I gave one to your father . . . in case he lost it."

I took it from him.

"We have to go," the driver said. "I have to get them there for their flight or they might miss their turn."

"I understand. Thanks for stopping."

The woman said something to her husband and he translated. "My wife said your father and brother were such good swimmers, and they were strong. She said she is sure they must be fine and that maybe they are still there helping people."

Right—it was like I had imagined. I knew it. They wouldn't have been able to just walk away if people needed their help.

The truck started up with a loud rumble and a puff of blue smoke shot out the exhaust.

"Your family will be in our prayers," the man said.

"Thank you."

The truck started to move.

"God bless your family!" he yelled out.

The truck picked up speed and the man and his wife waved as it rocked up the road. I waved one more time and then turned and started walking again.

My head was filled with thoughts. I tried to do some mental arithmetic, tried to figure out the significance of everything I'd just heard. My whole family was alive after the first wave. My brother and father were down at the beach when the second wave hit, but my mother was probably up in the lobby. My father and brother were good swimmers. So was my mother, but not with the MS in relapse. They might have been separated, and it might have taken time for them to find one another. They had been helping and probably were still helping other people. The phones were down and that's why they hadn't called. I played it all around in my head. Had the odds increased or decreased? Was it more likely they were alive or less likely? What did it all mean? Nothing. It meant nothing until I found them.

I went to put away the picture, but stopped and looked at it one more time: the four of us, my father's arm around my shoulders, my mother beside me and my brother beside her with that stupid smirk on his face— why couldn't that boy ever smile? With everything that happened all the time—school and my father's job and swimming and sports and friends—it was as though there was never time for all four of us to be together. In fact, that photo marked the last time we'd all stood still in one place long enough to have a picture taken. And now . . .

I put the picture back in my wallet. I didn't have time to stand still.

The closer to the beach I got, the more people I saw. Most of them were locals. Some of them were pushing wheelbarrows or carts or carrying heavy loads on their backs. I didn't ask, but I thought I knew. Whatever they carted was everything they had. These were the few scavenged remains of the lives they had been living.

Up ahead I caught my first glimpse of the water. From what Steve had told me I knew I just had to keep to the right when I came to the roadway along the ocean. The resort would be in that direction. I was pretty sure I'd even recognize the intersection, because we'd traveled this way. It was the route we always took when we drove along the coast to go sightseeing inland.

I stopped on a little hill overlooking the scene below. Something was wrong. This wasn't the intersection I knew. There should have been dozens of little shops and roadside stalls all along that intersection, as far as the eye could see. I couldn't see anything. That meant I didn't know where I was or how far I still had to go or . . . I looked harder. There was nothing except debris. Along with flattened trees, logs, and branches, I saw boards and siding and galvanized tin scattered around . . . all the things that would make up those little wooden stores. This *was* the intersection I knew, it was just that everything I remembered was gone.

I continued along the road, down the hill toward the ocean. The scene was beyond words. What had once been a thriving, living, vibrant place was almost completely gone. There were a few people poking through the rubble, searching for something or someone. On the road there were a couple of bicycles and a smattering of people, moving slowly, trying to get through and over the wreckage that overran the road. Patches of black asphalt were visible, but the road was almost buried in sand. It was as if the beach had overrun the road, and I guess, in some ways, it had. The ocean had exchanged stores and trees for sand. Sand and boats. Scattered among the snapped-off trees, on their sides or simply sitting perfectly upright, were fishing boats. The ocean had brought them up onto the land and then left them behind when the water had finally receded. They looked like toys left on the beach by some giant kid who'd tired of playing with them.

I moved slowly along the road, stepping over debris, moving through the sand. There were branches and whole logs tossed haphazardly across the road, and boards and a few bricks, and scattered among those were bright pieces of material—clothing. Had these been washed right off someone's back, or were they what remained of somebody's luggage, or had they been for sale in one of the little roadside stores?

Up ahead, the road was completely blocked by a bus tipped onto its side. Up close I could see that all of the windows had shattered, but the broken glass had been washed away. Inside, the bus was partially filled with sand. What had happened to the passengers and the driver? Hopefully they'd all made it out before the wave hit. I moved around the bus. Beyond it was a mangled bicycle, trapped underneath a car that was sitting on its roof, the side windows up and the windshield smashed out.

As I walked I looked on both sides of the road, trying to pick out something that I knew. Nothing was familiar. Whatever stores or stalls had been there were gone. The people were gone. Everything was gone.

Then, up ahead, I saw one of the hotels. It was ocean-side, ten stories tall. I could see the sign on its side, up at the top. I knew that sign well. There was one on each side of the building. I used to see it, bright and neon in the night sky, when I stood in front of our bungalow and looked way up the beach.

My parents hated that sign. They hated the hotel. I remembered how upset they were when it was built because they thought it took away from the character of the beach and the town. Now all I could think of was how people up on those higher floors would have been fine. They would have been like those people shooting video, the ones I'd seen on television, just watching, safely above the tsunami. Not like people in a bungalow.

The hotel gave me something to aim for. It was probably about halfway between where I now stood and our resort. It meant I knew where I was. I had a place to start.

I soon began to see a pattern. On one side of the road, the side away from the ocean, there was almost complete devastation. The stores and stalls and little houses that belonged to the locals had all been totally destroyed. On the other side sat the resorts. They were taller and made of concrete and bricks and they still stood. I was close enough to know there was damage—broken windows on the main floors all boarded up and yellow tape across entrances, doors missing—but these buildings were at least still standing. I knew the waves had been as high as thirty feet. That was like three stories tall, but there were four floors to our resort. All my family would have had to do was get to the top floor and they would have been fine. And even if the wave had caught them they could have kept swimming until they reached the top floor. They were all good, strong swimmers. I looked over at another car on its side. Were they strong enough to survive that kind of force? Was Mom?

Up ahead, just off to the side of the road, were two elephants. At first I thought they were just standing there, but as I got closer I could see they were working. Each had a man riding him—they called them mahouts, I knew—and on the ground were half a dozen other men. There was another bus on its side. They'd attached chains, and now the elephants were pulling, trying to get the bus onto its wheels. I stood well back, fascinated, and watched as they pulled it along, the mahouts yelling as the bus slid, the metal of the bus grinding, shrieking against the pavement. They got it to start to rock upright but then it fell back down with a crash. They kept pulling it along, the elephants backing up until first they left the road and then, at last, the bus was dragged clear as well.

Along this section of the road, the resort area, there was much more activity. Besides the elephants and the work crews trying to clear the road there were other people at work at the hotels. I could hear hammering and the sound of saws being used and I could see men working, clearing away debris but also trying to repair damage. I knew how important the tourism industry was to Thailand and how they needed the hotels to work again to get the tourists back. Strange, right now they were trying to get them all away to safety, but soon they'd want them to return.

Then I heard some men yelling—they'd been working beside the road cleaning and clearing, and one of them ran off. I was drawn over to see what was wrong.

That's when I saw my first body.

W
A
V
E

CHAPTER FIFTEEN

—

I wanted to look away, but I couldn't. The body was twisted and its upper half was completely encased in sand. The legs were mud-stained, the feet were bare. I decided it was a man; he was wearing shorts. He was probably Thai because he wasn't very big, almost like a boy . . . about the size of my brother.

One of the men came running back to the body. In his hands was a large pink tarp, made of the same kind of canvas used for kites or banners or tents. He laid it down on the ground and another two men started to dig, using shovels to try to free the body.

I stood there, stunned, watching. Part of me had the urge to run away. Another part wanted to yell out to them, tell them to be careful with the shovels, maybe even help dig with my hands. I tried to think. My brother wouldn't have been barefoot. He would have been wearing a pair of flip-flops, so that couldn't be—right, like the tsunami couldn't have taken those off his feet. Next I focused on the shorts. Was there a pattern beneath the caked-on, sandy mud? I moved closer, trying to see, but I couldn't be sure of anything.

One of the men dropped to his knees—he was using his hands to dig now. The second gripped a piece of metal that had been lodged in the ground, pulled it out, and tossed it to the side. Both men stopped. They grabbed the body by the legs and they began to pull! They strained, digging in their heels, their muscles bulging, until the body popped out and they tumbled over. I looked at the body. It wasn't Sam's.

Thank goodness. I realized that I'd been holding my breath and I inhaled deeply to fill my lungs. It wasn't my brother. It wasn't even a man. It was a woman. Other than the shorts, her clothes were gone. Her long, dark hair was matted with dirt and sand. Her eyes were closed, and there was a look of complete anguish on her face, as though she were in pain, or angry, or terrified. That was probably the way she had died.

The men picked up the body, one holding the legs and the other holding the arms. Gently they placed her on top of the canvas, and then they pulled the edges over so it covered her up. I turned away and started walking again.

Everywhere there was more of what I'd already seen: another boat well up on the shore, lodged between two shattered tree trunks; another car, this one on its roof;

boards and pieces of plywood; broken furniture; a bashed-up refrigerator; and more bursts of color, clothing half buried in the sand . . . was it just loose clothing or was I seeing the sleeve of a shirt that was still on somebody? I shuddered.

My attention was caught by flashing lights up ahead. I hurried along the road. There was a truck, something official with red lights on the top. It was the first official-looking thing I'd seen since I landed. There were lots of people crowded around and they were all standing in front of the remains of a small building. Only half of the store sign was visible, but there was enough left to show that it was a supermarket. Were they there to get food? Was the situation so desperate that people were scavenging for supplies?

I stopped at the edge of the crowd and peered over people's heads. The walls of the building stood but the roof was partially collapsed and the front windows were smashed in. A few steps led down into the store, which was filled with water. Debris floated on the surface— paper and some canned goods. And then a man popped his head out of the water. He started up the steps, pulling something behind him. It was a body. He dragged it, bouncing up the steps behind him, until three more men waded in and helped him carry it up. The three men were wearing masks, the type a doctor or nurse would wear.

The body was bloated and battered-looking. I was sure it was a man's, but I couldn't tell anything else. They placed him on a piece of bright-green canvas and started to wrap him up. I couldn't watch any longer. I had to get away.

I started walking again, but I needed to get off the road. There was nothing there but death and destruction. I cut down to the beach. I'd always loved just strolling along with the ocean beside me . . . I could only hope it would be better now than the road. I cut between two familiar hotels. Their once-beautiful manicured gardens were gone. Bushes, flowers, trees, even the grass—it was all lost, either ripped out or buried beneath a layer of sand. Now there was just sand and dirt and mud and puddles. There was a foul smell in the air, like rotting vegetation or putrid water.

I walked along the front path leading up to one of the hotels. The circular driveway was deserted and, strangely, it was clean and clear—no sand, no garbage, nothing. It was as if the tsunami had completely bypassed that one driveway. That didn't make sense. Somebody must have cleaned it already.

The windows and all the front doors leading into the lobby of the hotel were boarded up. Looking up, I could see that the second-floor windows were also broken, but they weren't boarded. Above that, the windows on the third and fourth floors were fine. If I looked only at the top of the hotel it appeared as if nothing was wrong.

I circled the building. I could hear noises— hammering—but couldn't see anybody. Around the side of the building, where there used to be gardens and seats and a patio, there was a giant pile of garbage. Somehow the wave must have simply left everything right there, pushed up right against the building. Just then a television set came flying out of an upstairs window and landed on the pile with a loud crash, sending pieces flying up into the air! They were cleaning out the rooms, the same way they'd already swept the front driveway. They were already trying to get things back to normal.

I walked in a wide arc around the pile, making sure that I was far enough away from the building to avoid anything else that might be tossed out.

Soon I was on the lip of the beach, and what had once been pristine, clean, open sand was now littered with garbage. The only thing that seemed untouched was the ocean itself.

I moved down until I was walking along the edge of the water, with the breaking waves washing up at my feet. I suddenly felt anxious. Here I was right beside the ocean. This was where people were—where my father and brother might have been—when the tsunami hit. I looked out at the water. It was brilliantly blue, with just a few gentle waves showing white edges as they broke against the shallows. Birds soared overhead, white against a cloudless sky. On the horizon there were fishing boats. It looked like a postcard. So perfect. So beautiful.

I tried hard to imagine the wave, a wall of water, rising higher and higher and crashing on the beach and . . . I couldn't do it. I'd seen the devastating results, even proof of the deaths, but I couldn't picture the ocean rising up to cause it.

Just up ahead was our resort. It seemed familiar and

foreign all at once. The hotel still stood. Solid, concrete, four stories high. From this distance it looked no different—except for what surrounded it. The trees that had once circled the pool had either been torn out or snapped in two, leaving shards sticking up. I knew the gardens and flowers would all be gone. It had once been so beautiful, and now it was just . . .

I stopped mid-thought and froze in place. That wasn't the only thing that was missing. The bungalows—the bungalows were gone. I looked up and down the beach, thinking that somehow I must have been so distracted that I'd just passed them, but there was nothing. Nothing whatsoever. Roofs, walls, windows, doors—everything gone. The trees and bushes, the paths leading up to them. Nothing. I searched the ground, desperately looking for a trace.

I picked up a board. Was it from one of the bungalows? There was a piece of corrugated metal . . . from a roof? No, the bungalows had wooden roofs with palm leaves for shingles. If I searched, would I find a trace of *our* bungalow? Would I find one of my father's T-shirts, or a skirt that belonged to my mother . . . or my brother's body?

I couldn't stay there any longer. I staggered up the beach and onto the patio. There had to be somebody here who could help me, who could tell me what had happened to my family.

I walked into the lobby—or what used to be the lobby. Inside was a mess . . . and there was a car lying bizarrely on its side against a wall. It was dark and damp and smelled awful. The place where I'd spent so much time, so many happy holidays, was barely recognizable.

Then I had a chilling thought. That man in the truck had said he thought my mother had been in the lobby. So, she might have been here, right here, when the second wave hit. How could she have gotten out? How could she have survived?

I couldn't stay there anymore. There was nothing. Nobody. Not my family, not staff, nobody. It was like standing in the middle of a haunted house. I had to leave.

I walked out the front entrance, through the frame where the door used to be, onto a carpet of sand. Mounds of garbage stuck out of the mud or rested in tangled, mangled piles.

"Hello . . . how are you?"

I turned. There was a man. He was older, with gray hair, dressed in shorts and a dirty shirt. He was a foreigner, a tourist.

"I'm looking for my wife," he said. "Her name is Aggie. I'm wondering if you have seen her." He showed me a picture of a smiling grandmother. "I wasn't here when it happened," he explained. "I was up in the hills on a hike . . . she didn't want to come . . . she was too tired. If only . . ." He started to cry.

"I'm so sorry . . . I haven't seen anybody. I'm looking for *my* family, for my parents and my brother." I pulled out the picture and showed it to him.

He wiped away his tears and took the picture from me. His hand was shaking badly. He shook his head.

"I've been searching since it happened . . . I've looked everywhere . . . everywhere."

"I just arrived, a few hours ago. I don't even know where to look."

"Have you been to the message boards?" he asked. "That's where you should start."

"I saw one at the airport in Bangkok. Are there boards here?"

"Yes, yes, there are boards and lists. You need to go and look."

"Where do I go?"

"Up the hill. Do you know where the temple is?"

"Yes. I've been there before."

"There are messages there from survivors, lots of messages. I've even seen people reunited right there, each looking for the other."

That sounded now like the kind of miracle I could only pray for.

"And there are pictures," he added.

"You mean, like, pictures of family members? I only have this copy."

He hesitated. "No, the pictures . . . they've posted pictures of the people they've already buried."

"Buried? What do you mean?"

"Some of the bodies have already been buried," he said. "The heat . . . disease . . . they had no choice but to put them in the ground. They took pictures of the people they couldn't identify. The pictures are all posted. It's mainly foreigners, tourists. It's awful, but I had to

W
A
V
E

163

look at them. My wife wasn't there . . . thank God, she wasn't there."

It seemed like such a small thing to be grateful for now—to find that your family's names were *not* on the list of the dead and buried—especially compared to the reunion I'd been hoping for. But *hope* was the key word— I couldn't give up now.

"Many people have been taken to hospitals and medevac clinics," he told me. "I'm going to check them next."

"Maybe I should go with you."

"No. The hospital is not close. You have to try close first. I'd go with you . . . I'd bring you, but I have to keep looking." He took both of my hands in his. "You'll find your family, and I'll find my wife. We have to keep looking, we can't give up."

I nodded and tried to fight back tears. He let go of my hands and walked away. I didn't know exactly where he was going, but I knew where I had to go.

The walk up the hill to the temple was tiring. I stopped on the way and ate two of the energy bars Steve had given me and drank an entire bottle of water. It was hot and humid, and I was thirsty and hungry, but I really needed to sit down and think. Everything I'd seen was swirling around in my head. How could all of this, how could *any* of this be real?

Up the road there were message boards that might hold the key, tell me where my family was, what had happened to them, for better or worse, and now, with the hilltop almost in sight, I hesitated. I guess it was almost better to believe there was a chance than to go and find out that all hope was gone. But to stay here, on the road, and not go any farther made about as much sense as simply staying in New York. Maybe less.

I heard a truck coming up the road. I stood up. The truck rounded the corner. It was an SUV with lights on the top—the vehicle I'd seen at the supermarket. Slowly it rumbled by, and the driver nodded to me as it passed. On the back were bright canvas bags—tarps, body bags. There had to be ten or twelve of them, stacked up like fireplace logs. Those bodies were going where I was going: the temple. I'd been there before, with my mother. She loved it. She always said it was a peaceful place, a place where she could think about what was really important to her. Now, I didn't want to go. I didn't want to be here. I felt so small, so alone.

I looked down at my phone. That was my only lifeline to the real world, to people I knew, people who could help me. I just wished it would ring. I could try to call Tad again. And tell him what? That I didn't know anything? There was no point. Not now. I had to go.

I made it to the top of the hill and joined the crowd. Most of the people there were locals, but there were lots of foreigners as well, all gathered around the message boards. I joined them in reading the messages. At first I was encouraged. So many people had lived and left behind their words, trying to connect with somebody. But for everybody who had lived there was a message looking for somebody who was lost. Maybe those people had just been separated in the chaos. Or maybe they were dead.

Then I saw the photos of the buried. The first showed a woman, old and gray, her eyes open, the color drained from them, an expression of such fear on her face that it looked as if she could have been scared to death. I felt like a stranger at somebody else's funeral.

I moved down the board, glancing at photo after photo of people who were dead. Some of the faces looked peaceful, as if they were simply asleep. Others were so bloated or bruised or so bashed in that it was hard even to tell if they were male or female; those I had to look at more closely. Photo by photo I moved down the line, each time praying I wouldn't see my family, and each time my prayer was answered. The board ended and they weren't there. That meant that they weren't buried. I allowed myself to see a small glimmer of hope.

Then I looked up and saw the courtyard in front of the temple. There was row upon row of brightly colored tarps. Bodies.

CHAPTER SIXTEEN

—

I stood looking at the courtyard. As I watched, another body was taken from a truck and carried in by four men, one at each corner. They lowered it gently to the ground at the end of one of the rows. Two Buddhist monks, wearing bright orange robes, walked among the bodies. They were chanting and banging on drums.

There had to be over a hundred bodies laid out in front of me. The canvases were colorful—blues and greens and even bright pink. It looked more like a circus than a morgue. If I hadn't known what was underneath those tarps, I might have thought that it was beautiful.

"Do you need some help?"

There was a man—a foreigner, a tourist—standing beside me. His voice was calm and his expression was gentle. I almost instinctively said no, but then thought better of it.

"I'm looking for my family. My mother and father and brother."

"You were separated from them when the tsunami struck?"

"No," I said, shaking my head. "I stayed home when they came here on holiday. I came down to search . . . from New York."

"I'm from California," he said. "I was here on holiday when it hit."

"And you're looking for somebody too?"

"Everybody in my party, my friends and I, we all got away safely. They're already heading home. I couldn't do that. There's too much here that needs to be done. I'm trying to connect those who need to be connected, and offering assistance to those who need help when there aren't any connections. Do you need to look?" he said, gesturing to the bodies.

I nodded.

"I'll come with you. My name is Seth."

"I'm Elizabeth . . . Beth . . . Beth Brooks."

"Hello, Beth."

He shook my hand. I'd never thought before about how much a handshake can convey, but his was warm, reassuring, sympathetic. I immediately felt grateful to him for sticking around. I needed help more than I wanted to admit.

"Beth, most of the bodies here are those of tourists. All are people who haven't been identified yet. Even people who were carrying ID that day were stripped of it by the force of the wave."

He led me in and we stopped in front of the first body. Once again he reached out his hand, and I took it.

"This first row is children, the middle row is females, and the last is males."

"The first row is longer than the others," I said.

"Children and old people were more likely to be killed than adults. Maybe because they couldn't run, or they didn't have the strength to hold on."

I thought of my mother, then, tried to picture her running when I knew sometimes she had trouble even walking because of the MS.

"Because of who you're searching for we have to look through all the rows. I'm sorry. I wish there were a better way to do this, but there isn't. I'm going to pull back the tarp and you look at the face," Seth said. "Some of the bodies are in rough shape, bloated or—"

"I've seen the pictures. I know."

"It's different looking at the person. You have to look hard to make sure. Sometimes people have trouble recognizing a family member, or maybe they just don't want to recognize them. You have to take your time."

He let go of my hand. He knelt down beside the first body and slowly pulled back the tarp. In a flash it revealed a very young, very blond girl. She couldn't have been more than ten or eleven. Poor kid. Poor family. Before I could even say anything he covered her back up. He knew I was looking for my brother.

We moved to the next body and he did the same. It was a boy, much younger, dark hair. I shook my head and he covered the body again. Body by body we moved. Some he passed over, and I realized why—the body under the tarp was too small to possibly be my brother. Some of them couldn't have been much more than babies.

He lifted up the tarp covering the last body in the row. It was a girl. She had short hair. Her eyes were closed and she looked so little, so peaceful, as if her mother had just finished reading her a bedtime story, kissed her on cheek, and she'd gone to sleep. Seth pulled the tarp back over her and the illusion was broken.

"Do you want to take a break?" he asked.

"Maybe just a minute."

He led me over to a small bench and I sat down.

"You should take a drink. I'll get you some water."

"No, I have some." I took off my backpack and pulled out a bottle. I was thirsty, but even more I wanted to take away the bad taste in my mouth. There was such a strong odor in the air . . . heavy and almost sickeningly sweet.

"I was just wondering . . . the smell . . ."

"That's mainly the disinfectant that they've been spraying on the bodies, but it's mixed with the incense from the temple. The monks are working hard to ease the path of the dead. Do you know much about Buddhism?"

I shook my head. "Not much. They believe in reincarnation, right?"

"That's part of it. They believe that in the moments after death, before the soul enters another life form, it is alone, scared, in turmoil. They feel that this is particularly true when the death has been sudden or violent. The monks are feeling overwhelmed as they try to bring comfort to these souls." He gestured with his hands. "So *many* souls."

"And the incense and the chanting and drumming are ways to comfort the souls?" I asked.

"That, and prayer and meditation."

We sat quietly for a moment until he asked, "Are you ready to continue?"

"I'm ready."

He led me over to the middle row. Again he bent down by the first body at the head and I stood at the foot.

"I know this is hard," Seth said. "Be brave, take your time, and if you need to stop we'll stop right away. Ready?"

I nodded, and he pulled up the corner of the tarp. There was a shock of bright blond hair and I gasped before I saw the face—it wasn't her.

"I thought for a second . . ." I explained. "She looks like my mother . . . I mean, the hair color."

He lowered the tarp over her again. "She's probably Swedish. So many Swedes," Seth said.

"My mother's family is from Sweden. I'm half Swedish."

"You don't look Swedish. The dark hair," he said.

"I got my father's hair. I always wished I had blond hair."

"Blonds have more fun. Isn't that what they say?"

"My brother has hair like my mother's. He looks Swedish."

I was struck by the strangeness of our conversation. We were standing in the middle of a morgue, in the courtyard of a Buddhist temple, in the middle of hundreds of bodies, searching for my family, and we were talking about hair color. Then again, maybe it wasn't so strange. Wasn't that how they identified bodies—hair color, gender, age?

"They've identified bodies from over forty different countries, but by far the most are from Sweden. Over three hundred deaths."

He moved to the next body and I took a position at the foot. This woman was heavyset, older, nothing like my mother, so there was no hesitation. Each time we looked at another body I held my breath as he pulled back the tarp, and each time it wasn't her. So many of the women were older. They were more the age of my grandmother than my mother.

My attention was caught by another couple at the far end of the makeshift morgue. The man had his arm around the woman's shoulder. They were in their early thirties. They were starting to look through the children's row. Were they looking for their son or daughter? How awful that would be . . . even more awful than what I was doing.

We finished the second row. My mother wasn't there either.

"Do you want to take another break?"

"No. I just want to get it over with."

"I understand."

One more row. One more terrible possibility. He lifted up the first tarp. The man was old, very old. His features were grizzled, his hair a tangled, muddy mess, and his eyes were wide open.

Somehow it didn't feel as awful now. In part, I'd just become numb. I'd looked at over a hundred bodies, held my breath each time as Seth pulled down the tarp, and each time it hadn't been them. Partly it was because now I was convinced that since neither my brother nor mother were here, then my father couldn't be here either. I realized that that logic wasn't very logical, but it made sense to me. They had to be all together. They were still all together. Not here. Maybe up at the hospital. Maybe in the airport in Bangkok. But not here.

Seth lifted up another tarp and my father's face looked up at me.

W
A
V
E

CHAPTER SEVENTEEN

"Just sit there," Seth said. "Breathe deeply and take sips of water."

I took another drink from the bottle. My whole body was shaking, and my legs felt so weak I didn't think I could stand even if I wanted to. When I'd realized that it was my father I'd almost passed out. My whole body got weak and my legs felt so rubbery that I just slumped down to the ground. At first I didn't even cry. I just sat there in shock. Then the tears came, and I didn't think they would stop.

Seth stayed there, holding my hand, not saying much of anything. Thank God he was there. To go through this all alone would have been even worse.

"Are you feeling a little bit better?" he asked finally.

"I just can't believe it . . . I can't believe that he's gone."

"I wouldn't even pretend to know how hard this is. Nobody who hasn't gone through it themselves possibly could. Could you do me a favor?"

What could I possibly do for him? I nodded.

"Tell me about your father."

"What?"

"Tell me about him. I want to know. Please."

"Um . . . he was a lawyer . . . I don't know what else to say . . . what do you want to know?"

"Was he a good husband and a good father?"

"The *best*. He always treated my mother so wonderfully, he loved her so much. And he was always there for me and my brother. He never missed a game or a piano recital or a school play. He always said he lived for his kids and . . ." I started to cry again.

Seth sat down right beside me and put an arm around my shoulder. "And that's why he's going to be missed so much."

I nodded and tried to fight back the tears. "It wasn't just his family. He was always trying to help people. Today a man on a truck told me that it was my father and my brother who saved the lives of his wife and son."

"I've heard so many stories of bravery, people risking their own lives trying to save others. I wonder if that's how he died, trying to save somebody. I guess we'll never know."

"My brother might know . . . if . . . if . . ."

"Until we know differently, your brother is alive. And so is your mother. You can't give up hope. Not yet.

You stay here," he said as he got to his feet. "I'll be back in a minute."

I sat on the bench and watched. All around me were other tourists, checking the message boards, showing pictures, or being led through the morgue. Twice I heard cries of joy as people were reunited. I watched, detached, as one couple embraced and jumped up and down with excited relief.

Then there were the tears of a different type. I sat there and watched as people found pictures on the board or a body under the tarps. They broke down sobbing, or screamed out in pain or in denial, howled as though they'd been physically wounded. It felt so unreal, as if I were watching a movie or the news on television rather than actually being there.

I should have felt happy for those who'd found somebody alive—ecstatic—and shared in the pain of the others who had not, maybe gone and tried to comfort them. Instead, I sat there, unable to think or feel or move. I just felt numb.

I envied the people who had somebody, to share either the grief or the joy. I had nobody. I'd never felt so alone in my life. If only there was . . . I reached for my phone and dialed my home number. I needed to speak to Tad, to ask him if he'd heard anything and to share what I knew. There was no signal. The phone was flat. Not even a busy signal.

Seth came back, with a cup in each hand. "There's been no reception today," he explained.

"But I got a call through earlier."

"Not from here. There are so many relay towers down that the service is really spotty. You can get a signal in a few places, but not a connection. Most won't even give you a signal. Here." He offered me one of the cups. "It's green tea. It's from the monks. Take it."

I took the cup.

"It's hot but good. Sip it slowly. I was wondering, other than that water, when was the last time you had anything to eat or drink?"

"I ate on the plane, and I've had a couple of those army ration bars."

"Not enough. You need to keep your own strength up. And do you know where you're going to sleep tonight?"

I shook my head.

"There's a temporary camp they've set up for foreigners. I'll arrange for you to get there."

"No, I can't go anywhere. I need to stay here . . . with my father."

"Beth, I can help you to identify him officially, but that's all. There's nothing more that you can do for him now. You have *other* work to do."

"You're right. I need to keep looking."

"You do, but first you need to get to the camp so you can rest, sleep, and get some food. It's only a tent, but you'll have shelter and something to eat."

"I don't need to stop, I'm okay."

"You won't be okay if you don't stop. Look, there are people there who can help. They keep track of all

W
A
V
E

the information, and new evacuees are coming in all the time. Who knows, your mother and brother might be there already."

"Do you really think so?"

"Lots of displaced foreigners are being gathered there before they get evacuated home."

"If I go there, will they make me leave, will they send me home?" I wasn't going to leave until I'd found Mom and Sam.

"Beth, I don't think anybody could make you do anything you don't want to do. Just go there and let them help you. Besides, it's a very hopeful place, the best place possible for them to be."

I knew what he meant. If I found my mother and brother there, it would be because they were alive and well.

They had to be panic-stricken worrying about my father. I just hoped Sam was being strong and helping Mom get through this. All this stress and hardship and lack of sleep would be playing havoc with her condition. As hard as this was for me, it had to be much harder for them. At least now I knew about my father. That meant that when I did find them I'd have to be the one to break the news. What would I say? How would I tell them?

"They've established satellite phone links at the camp so I know you'll be able to call home," Seth said. "You can let people know what happened, let them know if there's anything they can do to help."

"I'll call when I get there."

"Good. We have all the information we need here,"

Seth said. "As soon as a representative from the State Department comes through here again I'll make sure they know who your father is, that he's an American citizen, and they'll make arrangements to transport him back to the States."

"Thank you for doing that."

"And I have your cell and home phone number. If I hear anything I'll try to contact you. Here, take my number." He pressed a piece of paper into my hand. "You might not be able to get through, I don't know, but at least you can try to reach me if you need to. I just wish you weren't alone."

"Me too."

"There was one other thing," Seth said. "I was speaking to the Buddhist monks about your father. I told them that he was a good man, a good father and husband, and that he saved lives, possibly even dying while trying to save others. They asked if they could have your permission to help comfort his soul."

"What would they do?"

"They would pray, chant, beat drums, and light incense. They would leave small gifts by his body. By doing those things, the soul is calmed and reassured. It's a very beautiful ceremony."

"That would be nice."

"The monks said that they want to ease his discomfort. They believe that the dead wander, lonely and confused, until they are given calm and guidance. They said that your father accumulated a great deal of good karma in his life and they want to help him move to the next level."

"Tell them thanks for me."

"I'll tell them. Now we have to get you to the camp."

"Excuse me," a man said.

I'd noticed him already. He and a woman, holding a young blond toddler in her arms, had been moving around the temple, talking to people.

"We were wondering if either of you knows this child."

I shook my head.

"I don't know her," Seth said. "I just assumed she was yours."

"No," the woman said. The little girl had an arm around her neck and was clutching a little stuffed bear.

"Some locals brought her to us yesterday," the man said. "They found her abandoned, alone, and they asked if we could help."

"We don't even know her name," the woman continued. "We've been asking everybody, checking everywhere, looking at the boards, even posting her picture."

"She doesn't have many words, but the ones she has aren't English," the man added.

"She looks Swedish," Seth said. She had short, white-blond hair, blue eyes, and very fair skin.

"We thought so too. We've had people speak to her in Swedish."

"And Dutch and Polish and French and German. Nothing," the woman added.

"Maybe she's too young to speak," I suggested.

"Or too traumatized," Seth said. "I've seen some adults like that."

"We can't even turn her over to the authorities because we don't know which country she belongs to."

"We wouldn't do that, anyway," the woman added. "We couldn't just turn her over to strangers."

"I guess we'll just have to keep looking until somebody claims her," the man said.

"If somebody does claim that she's their child, you'll have to take all of them to the proper authorities," Seth said. "There have been rumors of people coming in and taking abandoned children."

"That's . . . that's . . . so hard to believe," the woman stammered.

"I've been told the same thing," I said. Steve the pilot had told me about that baby that four couples thought was their child.

"So you have to make sure that whoever says she's their child really is the parent. Okay?"

"Of course," the woman said. "Thanks for letting us know. Thank you." She squeezed the little girl tightly, and the toddler wrapped both arms around her.

"She seems to really like you," Seth said.

"I guess we're all she has right now."

"I'm going to arrange for a vehicle to take Beth up to the evacuation camp," Seth said. "How about if you three go along with her?"

A bit of company sounded pretty good to me.

W
A
V
E

"Thanks, but we heard about a hospital not far from here. We were going to try there next," the man said.

"You're right, it's not far. I could arrange for the vehicle to stop there before it takes you all to the camp."

"That would be great. Thanks."

"It's the least I can do. I just wish there were more." He turned to me. "Do you have only the one picture of your family?"

I nodded.

"Could I see it again?"

I took it from my pocket and handed it to him. He looked at it, long and hard, studying it. Then he handed it back.

"I won't forget your mother and brother. If they come here, I'll make sure you know. One way or another."

CHAPTER EIGHTEEN

—

As our SUV rumbled down the road, it stopped every time we passed someone who looked as though they might be a foreigner. The man and woman—he was Ryan and she was Lulu—would ask if the person knew the little girl. Not knowing her real name, they called her "Blondie." I'd then take the opportunity to show the same people the photo of my family.

Most often, the people we met would ask us about somebody *they* were searching for, or show *us* a picture. Once, both Ryan and Lulu thought they recognized a woman in a photo and they sent her husband back in the direction we'd come. They didn't want to get his hopes up for no reason, but they thought the woman in the photo—his wife—might be the one we'd seen sitting on the steps of the temple when we were leaving. Hope was all any of us had.

W
A
V
E

When we weren't looking out the windows I couldn't help but glance at the little girl snuggled into Lulu's arms. Lulu sang her lullabies and rocked her, and Ryan played peek-a-boo games. The little girl didn't seem to have words, but it wasn't that she was in shock or traumatized. She just didn't understand English. I was positive of that.

I was equally positive that she was fortunate that these were the people she'd been entrusted to. She wasn't their child, but they were going to protect her and comfort her as though she were. She was so lucky to have them. Maybe "lucky" wasn't the right word, though. Nothing here, nobody here would think this was *lucky*. But at least, through all of this, she had somebody.

"How old are you, Beth?" Lulu asked.

"Eighteen. I'm in first-year university. That's why I couldn't be down here with my family."

I explained to them about my family's holiday tradition, about my swim meet and why I'd decided to stay back in New York. I didn't say anything about my father, but I'd seen Seth pull them aside to speak to them before we left, and I was pretty sure he'd told them. I had a feeling that he'd also asked if they could keep an eye on me. I didn't mind that, either. Funny how, not so long ago, I'd wanted so badly to prove to my parents how independent I could be, and now here I was latching on to anyone who could offer me the least bit of help and support.

"We were wondering," Ryan said, "if you'd mind staying with us. That way, we could all search together. We'll try to find the family of the baby, and you can try to find your family. It might go better if we all work together as a team."

"It would really help us," Lulu said, "to have another set of hands. I don't know very much about children."

"I don't think you really need my help," I told them, "but I'd sure appreciate it if I could stay with you."

"Then we have a plan. Thanks for helping us find Blondie's family."

The SUV came to a stop in front of a small brown building made of wood.

"This is the hospital," the driver announced.

"Doesn't look like much," Ryan said.

I had to agree. It looked more like a small, cheap motel than a hospital, except that all along the path leading up to it were people sitting on chairs, slumped on the ground, or lying on makeshift beds. They had casts, or bandages on their heads, or IV lines dripping into them. The hospital must have been so full that patients had spilled out onto the path.

"I have to go and pick up some other people," the driver said. "I'll be back here within an hour to get you and take you on to the evacuation center. I'll meet you right here."

"Good. Thanks for the drive," Ryan said.

I hopped out of the vehicle, and Lulu struggled to climb out with the little girl in her arms.

"Would you like me to take her?" I asked.

"Thanks." She offered the girl to me, but Blondie spun around and clung tightly to Lulu, protesting, refusing to leave her arms.

Ryan had climbed out now, and he took Lulu's hand and pulled them both out together.

"She doesn't even want *me* to hold her," he said.

"She just wants to be in my arms," Lulu said. "I guess that's a good thing. I understand what Seth said about being careful, but she's not going to let anybody take her that she doesn't know."

We started up the path. There was no need to talk to the first people we passed because they were all Thais. Not my family, and obviously not little Blondie's, either. We stopped at a counter just inside the main door. Behind it was a Thai woman in a white uniform—a nurse, I hoped.

"Can I be of assistance?" she asked.

"We're looking for some people," Ryan explained.

"We have lists, but they are very incomplete," she replied.

"Even if they were complete it wouldn't help. We don't know the name of this little girl. We're looking for her family. Has anybody reported a missing child?"

"Many people are missing children, but our list includes only the people who are here, and, as I said, it's not very up-to-date. The best thing you can do is simply walk through the wards and ask. I wish we were more organized, but we're all doing our best simply to cope with the scope of the tragedy."

"We understand," Ryan said. "Where should we start?"

"Start with the wards. There are three of them. The cafeteria has been converted to a fourth. Out back, under a large tarp, we have a fifth area. And, of course, look in the corridors as you pass and check out the smaller rooms. I think we have a few patients in the laundry room right now."

"Thank you," Lulu said. "We'll start looking."

"Ready or not, here we come," Ryan added.

The nurse looked confused.

"Hide-and-seek . . . that's what you say."

She looked even more confused, but she nodded her head politely.

We started down the first corridor. Right away we saw people sitting on the floor. They didn't look injured—no bandages or IVs or casts—but they did look exhausted. Maybe they were waiting for somebody who was getting treated or had been admitted.

Lulu would try to get the attention of a few people at once and then ask about little Blondie. If people spoke English they would answer, while others just shook their heads. Some people didn't say anything—either they didn't speak English or they didn't understand it—but obviously they would have reacted if Blondie had been their relative or a child they at least knew.

I followed behind. For me it was easier. I knew who I was looking for, and neither of those people was there.

We entered a ward. This was more like what I had expected to find: rows of beds with bright white sheets and a shiny linoleum floor. A nurse in a clean, starched uniform was moving among the patients, and another woman in scrubs was pushing a man in a wheelchair. All the beds were filled, and I could see that almost all of the patients were foreigners.

Lulu walked up to the first bed. "Hello, do you know this little girl?"

The woman looked up. "No . . . no . . . don't know . . ." she said in broken, accented English.

"What language do you speak?" Ryan asked.

"Croatian."

"Could you speak to her in Croatian?" Lulu asked. She came closer and turned Blondie to face the woman.

The woman said something, a few sentences, and we waited for a reaction or response. Nothing.

"Sorry," the woman said. "Not Croatian . . . maybe Swede."

"We've tried that. She's not Swedish."

"Poor little baby," the woman said sadly. "So many lost . . . so many." She looked as though she was going to burst into tears.

"Thanks for trying," Lulu said.

We continued down one row and came back along the other. I followed behind, showing my family photo. Some people just shook their heads. Others asked questions or even reached out and took my hand, offering sympathy or encouragement to keep going, to not give up hope.

That was the hardest. I *was* starting to lose hope. My father was gone—I still had trouble believing that was real—and my mother and brother were lost. If they were alive, why hadn't they called somebody, why weren't they on a list, why hadn't we connected, why didn't anybody even recognize them? I had to keep looking, but what I really wanted to do was curl up in a little ball and go to sleep. Maybe that was what I needed. I could sleep and then get up in the morning, filled with more energy and hope, and start looking again.

"That's strike one," Ryan said as we exited the first ward.

The next corridor was filled with people, and the wall was lined with makeshift beds. Ryan and Lulu kept asking questions and I kept showing my photo.

We stopped at a man with his eyes closed. He had one arm in a cast and a line dripping into his other arm from an IV bag on a pole. He was asleep—or unconscious.

"Should I wake him up?" Ryan asked Lulu.

"I think so. We can't take a chance."

"Excuse me," Ryan said as he gently nudged the man. He didn't move or open his eyes. Ryan looked up at Lulu.

"Give him a little shake," she suggested.

Ryan pushed his shoulders and the man opened his eyes. He looked groggy, half asleep, or so heavily medicated that he wasn't all there.

"Sorry," Ryan said. "Do you know this girl?"

The man opened his eyes wide. He looked confused, frightened. He looked at Blondie and then at me.

"Do you know her? We're looking for this little girl's family?"

He muttered something in a language I didn't understand and then turned to face the wall.

"I guess that's a no," Ryan said. "I hated doing that. Poor man looked to be in a lot of pain."

"There was no choice," Lulu replied. "We owe it to Blondie and her family."

We walked into the second ward. It was almost identical to the first, orderly and organized, so different from the corridor—so different from what was outside the doors.

Ryan explained the situation to the first two patients, two women who would have been about the right age to be Blondie's mother. One answered in English. The other just shook her head, her expression so sad that I felt like crying. I couldn't help but wonder who she'd lost or who she was still looking for. I looked away from her. I didn't want to imagine anybody else's tragedy.

"Hello," Lulu said to the next woman. "I was wondering if you knew this—"

"*Teti*! *Teti*!" Blondie squealed. She was reaching over Lulu's shoulder and scrambling, trying desperately to get out of her arms. "*Teti*!" She reached out again.

"*Baiba*!" a man cried from a bed on the other wall.

Lulu let the struggling Blondie down and the little girl ran right across the floor. We ran after her. She practically threw herself at the man, who wrapped his one good arm around her. His second arm and one leg were encased in plaster.

The man started crying and speaking, while Blondie buried her face in his chest and wrapped her arms around him tightly.

He looked up at us. "*Ta ir mana meita . . . mana meita!*"

"We don't understand . . . we don't know what you're saying."

"My daughter . . . this is my daughter . . . my Baiba . . . we thought she was . . . she was . . ." He started to cry again and hugged her even tighter.

"*Mara! Nac! Nac! Mara!*" he yelled at the top of his lungs. What was he saying? What was he doing?

A nurse came running over, and then a porter. A woman pushed past them and she threw her arms around Blondie and the man, and I knew—this was the mother! This was Blondie's mother!

"I don't think we have to check for identification," Ryan said.

Lulu started to cry, and Ryan wrapped an arm around her. I started to cry as well, and they both hugged me. We all watched—the whole ward watched, dozens of people gathering around—while the three of them sobbed and hugged and talked in whatever language they were speaking.

The man looked up at last. He reached out and took Lulu's hand and pulled her—pulled all of us—forward. The woman stood and hugged each of us.

"You have done . . . done . . . my English is no so . . . you have given back my life," the woman, the mother, said, and she started sobbing again.

"She was in my wife's arms when the wave over-whelmed her," the man said. "She was lost . . . drowned . . . gone. How did this happen? How is she here?"

"She was brought to us by locals. We cleaned her up and started searching for her family. We didn't even know her name."

"Baiba, her name is Baiba. My mother's name."

"I heard her say that word, I think," Lulu said. "We just couldn't understand what she was saying."

"What language are you speaking?" Ryan asked.

"Latvian . . . we are from Latvia."

"Across the Baltic from Sweden. We thought she looked Swedish."

"Her grandmother, my wife's mother, is Swedish."

Like my mother, I thought.

Blondie—Baiba, now—snuggled into her father's chest.

"This is a miracle," he said. "You have brought us a miracle! I do not know how we can ever repay you."

"You already have," Lulu said.

I knew what she meant. In this tragedy, in this unbelievable, unfathomable tragedy, with hundreds of thousands of people killed, many more injured, buildings destroyed, lives changed forever, this miracle that had taken place. And I was a little part of that miracle. Maybe that was all I could expect, and it would have to be enough. A second miracle was more than anybody could hope for.

"Beth."

I looked at Ryan and Lulu.

"Beth."

It wasn't them. I stared across the aisle. My brother looked back at me and he smiled.

CHAPTER NINETEEN

—

I stood on the beach holding my brother's hand. He was so much steadier on his feet than he'd been only three days before, and to look at him you wouldn't have known how close he'd come to dying. The doctors had told me that he was unconscious for almost a full day after he was brought in—a blow to the head—and even the following day he'd barely made sense when he spoke. It was only a few hours before I'd found him— before he'd found me—that he'd been able to give his name. There was still a nasty bump, the size of an egg, on the back of his head. He said he remembered getting hit by the second wave, being torn away from our father, and then something hitting his head. Nothing else. He didn't even know how he got to the hospital. The last time he'd seen our mother, he said, she was in the lobby of the resort, helping. He had no idea what might have happened to her.

When I'd found him I'd cried more than I ever had before. I cried tears of joy at finding him, but also tears of sadness for my father, for my mother, for everything I'd seen or heard, for everybody who had lost a life or a loved one. But still maybe most of all for my brother. I'd found him.

The next three nights I slept in a chair beside his hospital bed. Ryan and Lulu offered to stay with me, keep me company, but I told them I was okay. I had someone now—I had Sam. I kept finding myself reaching out, just to touch him, even when he was asleep. I'd wake up in the middle of the night in that chair and just lean over so I could put a hand against his shoulder. I needed to know that he was there and breathing, by my side. I just needed the contact. I think he needed it, too.

It was hard to leave him, especially that first morning, but I knew I had to keep looking for my mother. That was how I spent the days. Searching. For that first day and the next I felt hope. She wasn't on the lists of the dead, no picture on the boards, and she wasn't under a tarp in any of the morgues. But she also wasn't at the evacuation center, or at the camp, or at the hospital. She hadn't called. And I knew. She hadn't called because she couldn't.

Slowly I had to recognize in my heart what I'd known for some time in my head. My mother was gone. She was one of the thousands who were missing but would never be found. She was buried in a collapsed building or under tons of sand and mud, and her body wouldn't be uncovered for days or weeks or even longer. Or maybe she had been pulled back out to sea with the retreating water. I still held on to a little hope, a dream of another miracle, but, really, I *knew.*

In a strange way, I was grateful that I didn't have to share with her what had happened to Dad. It would have broken her heart in two. Telling my brother about our father was the hardest thing I'd ever done in my whole life—harder even than finding him under that tarp. The next hardest thing was helping Sam to understand that my mother was gone, too. It was just the two of us now. All we had was each other.

The sun was just getting ready to sink into the sea as we stood on the beach. Surrounding us were a handful of tourists, other foreigners, as well as dozens and dozens of local people. Everybody there had lost somebody. Some had lost everybody.

"It's beautiful here," Sam said.

I was startled out of my thoughts. "Yes, it is."

"Hard to believe . . . any of it."

"It is."

My brother hadn't said much in the last few days. There was too much for him to understand, to accept. It was too much for me too.

Tomorrow morning we'd be flying home. My aunt and uncle would be waiting for us at the airport in New York. Tad would be there, too. I wasn't sure what was going to happen to Sam and me—where we would live, what we would do—but I knew we had a home with my aunt and uncle for as long as we wanted. We'd have to arrange a funeral service for my father and mother, sell the house, and maybe I'd have to take a semester off school to help my brother settle into their home and a new school and—there was no point in even trying to think it through. There'd be time, and I'd have help. Right now I just had to be here, with Sam.

I looked over at my brother as he stared out at the water. He looked as sad and solemn and serious as I felt . . . as the occasion deserved. I squeezed his hand tighter.

Moving among us on the beach, drifting as if they were orange sails pushed by the gentle wind, were the Buddhist monks. Their voices were soft and calm, chanting words that I didn't understand. All around us there were candles set into little holes dug in the sand. They provided puddles of light that slowly spilled over and onto the beach, and as the sun began to set, its rays were replaced by their warm light.

One by one people walked down to the water's edge. There they lit a candle, which was placed on a small paper boat. The boat was then released and it drifted out to sea, carried by the wind and the receding tide. There was already a fleet, an armada of little boats heading out from the shore, following one another into the darkness.

The monk handed me a candle. He offered one to Sam, and he hesitated, and I knew why.

"We're not giving up," I said. "It's to light the way for her to come back to us."

Neither of us could fully give up on that last grain of hope.

The monk held out his candle to light ours. "From one flame a thousand candles may be lit," he said, "to be reborn in a higher form."

I placed the candle on the little boat. It was so delicate, so fragile. Sam did the same. Carefully we pushed the boats out into the water, and as the wind captured their paper sails they hurried along. The two boats caught those in front and were joined by others from behind until they all merged together, and I couldn't tell anymore which had been launched by us, or which was for my father and which was for my mother. But it didn't matter. They were out there, among a hundred boats, two hundred boats, all clustered and glowing. Together, they weren't so alone.

I looked over at my brother. I squeezed his hand again and he turned to me. Together, we weren't so alone, either.